"The memory is t[oo] [real to] be real."

At his words, Rachel grew still, almost as if she'd stopped breathing. "What memory?"

"You. Me. Together. Making love."

"That's ridiculous!"

"Is it?" Stephen asked. "Then why do I feel like more than anything I want to carry you into that bedroom and make love to you?"

"Don't be silly. We're like—"

"Brother and sister? I don't think so." In two quick strides he reached her and kissed her hungrily, tasting her sweetness, and experienced the heady sensation of coming home after a long absence.

Unable to resist, she leaned into his embrace. When his hands reached the bare skin of her midriff, she pulled away. "No," she cried. "We can't."

He drew in a lungful of air to steady himself. He'd loved this woman. He'd stake his life on it. "Look me in the eye and swear to me we've never been together, and I promise not to touch you again."

She shook her head. "It's not that simple. It's— Stephen, this is a mistake."

He pulled her toward him again. "I don't know much, Rachel," he said before his lips claimed hers again, "but I know this is no mistake."

ABOUT THE AUTHOR

Charlotte Douglas has worked as a college English instructor, an actress, a journalist and even a church musician, but she enjoys most creating romantic mysteries packed with suspense. She lives with her husband and two cairn terriers in a small town on Florida's west coast.

Books by Charlotte Douglas

HARLEQUIN INTRIGUE
380—DREAM MAKER
434—BEN'S WIFE
482—FIRST-CLASS FATHER
515—A WOMAN OF MYSTERY
536—UNDERCOVER DAD

Don't miss any of our special offers. Write to us at the following address for information on our newest releases.

Harlequin Reader Service
U.S.: 3010 Walden Ave., P.O. Box 1325, Buffalo, NY 14269Canadian: P.O. Box 609, Fort Erie, Ont. L2A 5X3

Undercover Dad
Charlotte Douglas

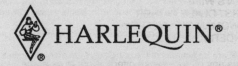

HARLEQUIN®

TORONTO • NEW YORK • LONDON
AMSTERDAM • PARIS • SYDNEY • HAMBURG
STOCKHOLM • ATHENS • TOKYO • MILAN • MADRID
PRAGUE • WARSAW • BUDAPEST • AUCKLAND

ISBN 0-373-22536-9

UNDERCOVER DAD

Copyright © 1999 by Charlotte H. Douglas

Visit us at www.romance.net

Printed in U.S.A.

CAST OF CHARACTERS

Stephen Chandler — an unforgettable FBI agent who can't remember who's trying to kill him.

Rachel Goforth — Stephen's ex-partner and a target of the same faceless stalker.

Jessica Goforth — Rachel's baby daughter.

Jason Bender — FBI agent and Stephen's friend, whose life also might be at risk.

Harold Maitland — Either an innocent victim or the mastermind behind his wife's kidnapping.

Bubba Tucker and Weed Fulton — Kidnappers with dangerous friends.

Ralph Fulton — Weed's brother.

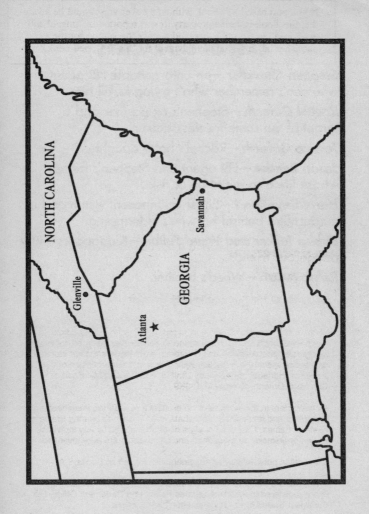

Prologue

"Rachel? Doc, is that you?"

Rachel Goforth grabbed the edge of the stainless steel counter and struggled for breath. The unexpected shock of Stephen Chandler's voice on the crime lab phone made her knees buckle, squeezed the air from her lungs, and forced her to admit again what she'd spent the past sixteen months trying to deny.

She missed him.

No matter that she hadn't seen or spoken with her former partner in over a year, not since she'd left the FBI in Savannah and joined the Cleveland County, North Carolina, Sheriff's Department. Even at a distance he had monopolized her thoughts and haunted her dreams.

For the past year, however, thanks to an answering machine at home and an assistant at work to screen her calls, she had managed to avoid talking to him. Today her assistant was out with the flu, and Rachel had answered the call herself.

"Stephen, what a surpri—"

"Don't talk."

"But—"

"Just listen. You alone?"

She flinched at the sharpness in his tone. "Yes, but—"

"You're in terrible danger, Rachel."

"What kind of—"

"Get out of there as fast as you can. Tell no one where you're going."

"Where *am* I going?" she asked with more than a hint of irritation.

"Do you have a secure fax line?"

Shaking off her confusion, Rachel gave him the number.

"I'm faxing you a map to a safe house in the mountains. Drive straight there *now*. Whatever you do, don't go home first or stop for *anything* along the way. Understand?"

"Yes, but—"

"No *buts*." A hint of panic, an emotion as alien to Stephen's easygoing personality as dry land to a fish, vibrated in the deep, warm voice she remembered so well. "I'll join you as soon as I can and explain everything. In the meantime, trust no one."

His uncharacteristic anxiety frightened her, and that fear triggered anger. "I can't abandon my job and rush off to the middle of nowhere without good reason. You have to tell me *something*."

"It's about a case we worked together in Savannah. That's all I can say now. Rachel, please. No more questions. Just *move*."

"But, Stephen—"

The line clicked in her ear. She replaced the receiver in its wall cradle and drew a deep breath.

What was going on?

If the bizarre warning had come from anyone else, she would have shrugged it off as a crank call. But Stephen Chandler had never been a man to panic, even under the worst circumstances. Not only an experienced investigator, one of the Bureau's best, he also possessed an unerring intuition that had solved dozens of cases and at one time had even saved her life. He wouldn't have warned her if danger didn't exist.

Nerves frayed by his strange request, she jumped when the fax line rang at the other end of the empty lab. The machine whirred and spit out a single sheet.

Stripping off her lab coat, she strode to the fax machine and removed a hand-drawn map from the tray. At her desk she yanked her purse from the bottom drawer and stuffed the map in its outer pocket. After a moment's hesitation she picked up her phone and punched in the extension number of Edith Watson, her boss.

"I have an out-of-town emergency that needs immediate attention," she said when Edith answered. "I'll have to take some personal time."

"Anything I can do?" Edith asked this in the gruff voice that made senior sheriff's detectives shake in their shoes, but Rachel could detect the underlying concern in her tone.

"My work's caught up, except for completing those slides for the Hambright case."

"Don't worry about work. I meant anything I can do for you?"

"No, thanks. I'll be away for a few days, that's all," Rachel improvised. She couldn't tell Edith her plans when she had no idea what they were. "I'll check in by phone. If you need me, leave a message on my home answering machine."

Rachel hung up the phone, grabbed her quilted jacket from the closet by the door and hurried outside. Taking flight ran against the grain of her calm, rational nature, but she trusted Stephen's instincts. Four years as his partner had convinced her that when Stephen sensed danger, trouble was definitely nearby.

The threat of imminent harm wasn't an impossibility. Between them, they had sent enough criminals to jail and foiled enough crimes that any one of hundreds of felons could be after them, out for revenge.

Cool, crisp October air filled her lungs as she strode across the parking lot. The vivid scarlet and gold of maples and hickories shimmered in the brilliant sunlight, but Rachel gave the spectacular autumn foliage only a passing glance. With a quick, practiced eye she surveyed the lot, climbed into her Explorer, and locked the doors, then shook her head at her jitters. If she was safe anywhere, it was in this lot filled with dozens of sheriff's deputies' marked vehicles.

Where was she headed?

She pulled Stephen's map from her purse and spread it across the steering wheel. The safe house he'd chosen was on a little mountain road near Glenville, west of Asheville. Taking Highway 74 at the bypass junction outside town would be the quickest route.

She started the engine and drove from the lot, taking a few random turns to see if she was followed. After several blocks, satisfied that no one tailed her, she headed back toward town.

Despite Stephen's forceful warning, she had to make one vital stop before heading west into the Smoky Mountains of North Carolina.

Keeping an eye on her rearview mirror and alert for suspicious vehicles, she thought back to the last case she and Stephen had worked together. Every detail was etched in her memory as if it were yesterday.

Chapter One

Rachel flexed her arms above her head, clasped her hands and stretched to relieve the kinks in her back. She had spent the past four hours at her word processor, typing reports on the week's assignments. When she joined the Bureau six years ago, she had envisioned exotic cases, dangerous missions and exhilarating investigations. What she hadn't foreseen was the avalanche of paperwork that snowed her under at the end of every week.

"What's up, Doc?" Strong hands grasped her shoulders from behind and massaged her tense muscles with expert, soothing motions.

Even if she hadn't recognized his voice, she'd have known Stephen Chandler stood behind her. Only Stephen called her "Doc," a teasing reference to the medical career she had abandoned to join the Bureau. To others in the office her nickname was "Scully," and their co-workers had dubbed Stephen "Mulder," another reference to television's fictional FBI partners on *The X-Files*.

She leaned gratefully into Stephen's ministrations. With his tall, muscular build, dark hair and eyes, and killer good looks, he was definitely as sexy and handsome as actor David Duchovny. But despite her petite figure and green eyes, she considered her ordinary appearance a far cry from the glamorous Gillian Anderson. She and Stephen had earned their nicknames, not from any physical resemblance to the actors, but from their respective specialties as forensics expert and hotshot investigator that paralleled the TV duo's expertise.

She glanced over her shoulder with a warm smile for her partner. "Starting in five minutes, I'm looking forward to a long, lazy summer weekend, without a single interview or case report in sight."

He kneaded her knotted muscles with strong, talented fingers, and she sighed with pleasure. Someday he was going to make some woman a wonderful husband. But not her. Their only other similarity to the television couple who supplied their nicknames was the depth and strictly platonic aspect of their friendship.

"Special plans?" he asked.

"Mmmmm." She leaned into his touch. "Sleeping late, then maybe a drive down to Jekyll Island to lounge on the beach. Want to come along?"

He bent forward to meet her eyes, arched his brows and grinned. "You inviting me to bed or the beach?"

She swatted him across his nose with her freshly printed report. "Be serious."

"Sorry to spoil your plans." Jason Bender, another of the agents assigned to the Savannah office, appeared before her desk. He ran a hand through his thick blond hair, a habit when he was nervous, and waved a pink telephone message memo. "You can cancel your weekend. Looks like the whole office will be called out for this one."

Stephen dropped his hands from her shoulders, stepped forward and propped a hip on the edge of her desk. "What have you got?"

"Kidnapping," Jason said. "One that'll blow the city wide-open if word gets out."

"Who?" Rachel asked.

"Margaret Dayvault Maitland."

"Margaret Maitland?" Rachel's long, lazy weekend dissolved before her eyes. A kidnapping was a life-and-death matter that put everything else on hold.

"You know her?" Stephen asked.

"Not personally," Rachel said, "but I know that her ancestors helped Oglethorpe found Savannah, and her parents, the Dayvaults, are the city's social and cultural icons. Surely you've seen theirs and Margaret's photographs in the local papers?"

"'Fraid not," Stephen said with a wry smile, "unless she plays for the Atlanta Braves."

Rachel rolled her eyes. "Then you probably didn't hear the nasty gossip, either. The city's bluebloods were horrified when the flower of Savannah's society became engaged to Yankee attorney Harold Maitland. They were even more appalled when she married him three years ago."

Jason's pleasant features crinkled in a grin. "They called him 'The Gucci Carpetbagger'—and that's the nicest thing they said about him."

"So what's the deal on his wife?" Stephen asked.

"We just got a call from Maitland," Jason said.

"He claims their car was forced off the highway south of Savannah Beach. Two armed gunmen kidnapped his wife."

"Is Maitland still at the scene?" Rachel asked.

Jason shook his head. "He said he was calling from home."

Stephen frowned. "Ransom demand?"

"Nothing yet," Jason said. "The kidnappers told Maitland he'd be hearing from them."

"Send a crime scene unit to examine the abduction location," Stephen ordered as senior agent, "and get a technical team together to set up phone taps at the Maitland mansion ASAP. Doc and I will interview the husband."

"You got it." Jason hurried toward his office.

Rachel glanced at Stephen, still perched on the edge of her desk. Frown lines wrinkled his wide forehead. "Something wrong?"

"A rich man like Maitland would have a cell phone in his car. Why didn't he report the kidnapping immediately instead of driving home first?"

Rachel shrugged. "Shock?"

"Maybe. But I have a funny feeling about this case."

Rachel's skin prickled. Stephen's "funny feelings" usually indicated trouble.

She shut down her computer and placed her report on the desk of the special agent in charge. Then, walking quickly to keep up with Stephen's long strides, she accompanied him out of the building to his car. In spite of her ruined weekend, adrenaline coursed through her veins. A fatal kidnapping was the reason she had left medical school and joined the Bureau, and although she gave her best to all her cases, any abduction, child or adult, received her special attention.

Twenty minutes later, Rachel and Stephen exited their car, parked across the street from the Maitland mansion. Opposite the attorney's house on the square was the Mercer House, scene of the infamous murder detailed in *Midnight in the Garden of Good and Evil,* which Savannah natives referred to simply as The Book. Since The Movie of The Book had been released, the square—in fact, all of Savannah—was clogged with curious tourists. Kidnappers could easily hide in the flood of strangers that inundated the city daily.

Stephen took Rachel's arm as they dodged tour buses to cross the street to the Maitland House. In the June afternoon, late sunlight streaming through moss-bearded oaks dappled the grassy lawns, and magnolias perfumed the humid air. In the shadow of a tall crepe myrtle, its branches bent low with deep-rose blossoms, a couple embraced in a passionate kiss.

Glimpsing them, Rachel experienced a momentary thrill of envy before her common sense kicked in. She'd been down that road several years ago and found only heartache and humiliation. Much better to have a reliable and undemanding friend like Stephen than a hundred unfaithful lovers.

They climbed the sweeping curve of stairs to the entry of the four-story Italianate house. Stephen rapped the heavy brass knocker against the thick, paneled door. A maid in a black uniform dress and crisp white apron answered, and they displayed their identification.

"Mr. Maitland's expecting you," the maid said. "He's in the drawing room. This way."

She led them to an arched doorway, motioned them inside and scurried down the hall out of sight.

At the opposite end of a room that appeared to stretch the length of the house, Harold Maitland stood at an antique sideboard and filled a cut-crystal glass with whisky from a Baccarat decanter.

"I'm Agent Chandler," Stephen flashed his ID, "and this is my partner, Agent Goforth."

"Thank you for coming so quickly." Maitland's raspy voice trembled with emotion. "Have a seat."

Rachel settled in a brocaded Louis XIV chair and watched with amusement as Stephen sat tentatively on a Chippendale settee, as if wondering if it would hold. The room could have been a museum with its lavish, antique furnishings. A gilded Empire mirror above a fireplace mantel of Carrera marble reflected the brass and crystal chandelier, an Ormolu clock ticked discretely on a side table, and Aubusson carpets in muted pastels covered gleaming hardwood floors. Everything from the oil-painted portraits and landscapes to the brocaded wall coverings whispered old money. Her attention fell on the largest portrait, Margaret Maitland in her wedding gown, and her amusement vanished. The woman's life was at stake unless they could locate and save her.

"Can I pour you a drink?" Maitland asked.

"No, thanks," Stephen said.

Rachel drew her attention from the elegant room to its owner and wondered how many drinks he'd consumed before their arrival. She shook her head at his offer.

"Southern 'Comfort.'" Maitland lifted his glass, swallowed its contents in one gulp and poured another.

In his early forties, Maitland's dark hair was thinning at the temples, gold designer eyewear framed pale gray eyes, and thin lips stretched over wide, gleaming teeth. Perspiration beaded his pallid skin, colorless except for a dark shadow of beard, and his hands shook noticeably. His wife's abduction had clearly shaken him.

Short and stocky, Maitland looked uncomfortable in his expensive suit that pulled across his shoulders and stomach as if he'd gained weight since its purchase. According to the information he'd given Jason when he phoned, his wife had been abducted over an hour ago, yet his silk tie remained knotted tightly at his starched collar, as if holding him together and under control.

"Tell us what happened," Stephen said, "every detail that you can remember."

The gentleness conveyed in her partner's voice was one of the reasons Rachel found Stephen so likable. Beneath his powerful physique and an attitude of unrelenting severity in dealing with criminals lay a core of warmth and compassion that made him extraordinary, not only in dealing with victims, but in being a friend.

At Stephen's words, Maitland relaxed before her eyes. He slumped into a chair that seemed too fragile to support his bulk and rolled the glass between his palms. "We were driving down to Brunswick to visit Margaret's cousin. South of Savannah Beach, on a deserted part of the highway, an old Impala forced us off the road. Two men jumped out. Both had guns. They threatened to kill us if Margaret didn't get out. As soon as she unlocked her door, one of them grabbed her and threw her into the Impala. The other man said I'd be hearing where to leave the ransom. Then he climbed into his car and they took off."

"Did anyone else know about your trip to Brunswick?" Stephen asked.

Maitland frowned. "What do you mean?"

"The kidnappers were waiting for you," Rachel explained. "How did they know you'd be coming that way?"

"Habit," Maitland said. "We visit Margaret's cousin every Friday."

Rachel nodded. The circle of suspects had just widened from acquaintances and employees to anyone who'd taken the trouble to stake out the Maitlands' movements over a period of weeks.

"Describe the Impala." Stephen drew a small notebook from the pocket of his suit jacket and clicked the nib of his ballpoint pen.

"Late seventies model. The paint was so faded, I didn't get a good impression of color—maybe blue."

"Did you get a look at the men?" Rachel said.

Maitland tossed down the remainder of his drink and set the glass on a mahogany side table, heedless of the polished surface. "White men. One was big, over six feet. He had to hunch down to talk to me through the car window."

"And the other?"

"Small, but wiry."

"What about their faces? Any distinguishing marks?"

"They wore ski masks." Maitland closed his eyes, as if remembering. "But one had a tattoo."

"Where?" Stephen asked. "What kind?"

Maitland pointed to his left elbow. "A spiderweb, an immense thing that covered several inches of his arm."

Rachel glanced at Stephen, and his eyes flashed with comprehension. They had investigated enough hate crimes to know the infamous spiderweb tattoo was the insignia of white supremacists who committed murder in their battle for ethnic superiority. If Maitland's description was accurate, they were dealing, not with bumbling amateurs, but very dangerous individuals.

Stephen glanced up from his notebook. "Do you own a cell phone?"

Maitland appeared confused. "Yes. Why?"

"Why didn't you call the police as soon as your wife was taken?"

Rachel, knowing this response was crucial, studied Maitland's face.

His eyes blinked rapidly behind the lenses of his glasses. "All I could think of was hurrying home, to be here when the kidnappers called."

His obvious nervousness told her nothing. He could be lying—or he could have been so concerned for his wife, his motive was exactly as he'd stated.

A rapping at the front door interrupted the interview. In a few seconds the maid appeared in the drawing room doorway. "It's more FBI, Mr. Maitland."

"That'll be the technical team," Stephen explained. "They're here to establish the phone taps and monitor incoming calls."

Maitland leaped from his chair, knocking over his glass in his excitement. "My God, they can't come here!"

"Why not?"

"If the kidnappers know I've contacted the authorities, they'll kill Margaret. They warned me."

"It's all right," Rachel assured him. "They're driving a caterer's van, and the equipment is concealed in catering coolers and baskets. If the kidnappers are watching, they'll assume you were planning a party and, in the excitement, hadn't bothered to cancel the plans."

"Where should we set up the phones?" Stephen asked.

Maitland swiped his hand across his receding hairline and sighed. "The dining room will probably accommodate their equipment best. It's across the hall."

The maid disappeared to direct the technicians. Maitland picked up his glass from the carpet and headed back to the sideboard.

"I'd go easy on the Southern Comfort if I were you," Stephen said gently.

Anger suffused Maitland's pale face with a flush of color. "You've got some nerve—"

"You'll need a clear head," Rachel said, "when the kidnappers call."

The attorney abandoned his glass and wiped his palms on the front of his jacket. "Of course. You're right."

"Who else knows about your wife's kidnapping?" Stephen asked.

Maitland wrinkled his forehead in thought. "Only

you—the FBI—and Margaret's parents. I called them after I alerted your office. They should be here soon."

Stephen nodded. "I want you to think very carefully. Do you have enemies?"

Maitland managed a wry smile. "Besides my in-laws?"

Rachel shook her head. "Anyone who might have taken Margaret for revenge?"

The attorney grew very still, and the sounds of low voices drifted from the dining room where the technicians worked. "You think they intend to harm Margaret?"

Rachel avoided looking at Stephen. They both knew the probability existed that Harold Maitland might never see his wife alive again.

"That's only one possibility," she said, "but we have to check every angle."

"Okay." Maitland took a deep breath. "Let me think. There must be dozens of people who have a grudge against me. Every attorney, whether he wins or loses a case, always ticks off somebody."

In the entry hall, the front door opened and slammed against the wall.

"Where is he?" a man's deep voice shouted. "Where's that Yankee son of a—"

"Parker, don't make a scene," another drawling voice, soft and cultured, interrupted.

Rachel and Stephen stood as an elderly couple swept into the room. The big man's face was florid beneath a shock of thick white hair, but the woman was a picture of composure, not a curl out of place beneath her elegant veiled cloche that matched her navy linen dress, her white gloves immaculate. Serena

Dayvault, a true steel magnolia, maintained the dress code of Savannah's elite even when her only daughter had just been abducted.

Rachel couldn't resist comparing Serena to her own mother. If Sally Goforth had learned someone had kidnapped her daughter, fashion and decorum would have been the last things on her mother's mind.

Parker Dayvault, not attempting to disguise his rage, strode across the room toward Maitland, looking as if he intended to strangle the man. "How could you allow this to happen?"

"Mr. Dayvault, please." Stephen's reasonable tone rang commandingly in the large room. "Recriminations won't help us bring your daughter home."

The towering man turned to Stephen. "Who the hell are you?"

"Special Agent Chandler, FBI. This is my partner, Agent Goforth. We have a team in place waiting for the ransom call."

Dayvault's bushy white brows lifted above his blazing eyes, and he turned back to his son-in-law. "That's why you called us so fast, isn't it, boy? Need somebody to write the check when that call comes in?"

"Parker, please." Serena's deceptively soft voice held a note of irrefutable authority. "Agent Chandler is right. If we want Margaret back, we must work together."

Parker thrust his big hands in the pockets of his golf slacks and glared at his son-in-law.

Serena pulled off her gloves, removed her hat and handed them and her purse to the waiting maid.

"Please," she said to the two agents, "be seated and tell us how we can help."

Stephen remained standing, and Rachel followed his cue. Serena Dayvault was obviously a woman who liked to take charge, but this was the FBI's investigation.

"When you arrived," Rachel said, "Mr. Maitland was trying to think of any enemies who might wish to harm him through his wife. Do you or Mr. Dayvault know anyone with a grudge against you who might try to harm your daughter?"

Serena pressed well-manicured fingers against her lips, and her lavender eyes flooded with tears. "You can't live as long as we have without making some enemies, but no one I know would resort to kidnapping...or violence."

Parker scowled at Maitland. "*You* have enough enemies to fill a camp meeting, boy. This is all your fault."

Stephen appeared ready to act as peacemaker again, but the bank of phones in the dining room began to ring. "Mr. Maitland, come with me. And don't pick up the phone until I signal you."

Rachel followed Stephen and the attorney across the hall into the dining room with the Dayvaults close behind. The technicians had shrouded the antique table, large enough to seat twenty, with a felt cloth to protect the finish. Its surface was covered with telephones and monitoring and recording equipment. Two technicians, wearing headphones, sat at the monitors. One nodded to Stephen and pointed to two phones at the end of the table.

"When you pick up," Stephen instructed the attorney, "keep them talking as long as possible." He gave the signal, and concurrently Rachel and Maitland lifted the receivers.

"Maitland?" a muffled voice asked.

"This is Harold Maitland."

"Listen good, 'cause I'm only saying this once."

"I'm listening."

"It'll cost you two million dollars to get your wife back in one piece."

Chapter Two

"Two million dollars?" Maitland looked ready to faint. "It's Friday evening. The banks are closing. I can't get that kind of money before Monday."

"Get the money," the man said with a snarl. "I'll call later with instructions where to leave it."

Stephen made a rolling motion with his hand, indicating Maitland should keep talking.

"It may take longer than Monday," the attorney said. "That's a lot of money—"

"If it takes longer, your wife's dead." The line clicked in Rachel's ear.

"Got him!" the technician shouted at the other end of the table and scribbled furiously on a notepad.

"Where?" Stephen asked.

"A pay phone at a minimarket off I-95." He passed Stephen the address.

Stephen finished his own notation, ripped a page from his notebook, and handed it to the technician. "Call in these descriptions to the local cops and Georgia State Police. Ask for a BOLO on the Impala."

"Bolo?" Serena said. "What's a bolo?"

"Be on the lookout," Rachel explained. "The Impala is the kidnappers' car."

"Rachel?" Stephen's gaze met hers. They'd worked together so long, he didn't have to ask. She knew he wanted her to check the pay phone on the interstate with him.

"Ready," she said.

Parker Dayvault was arguing loudly with Harold Maitland over the quickest way to obtain the ransom money when she and Stephen slipped out the front door. They darted across the street and climbed into Stephen's car. Twilight cast long shadows across the square, and the crowds of tourists had thinned, probably heading to area restaurants for dinner.

Stephen maneuvered the car into traffic and headed west toward Interstate 95. The dusky glow of evening backlit his elegantly sculpted nose, strong jaw and a lock of dark hair tumbling over his broad forehead. If she hadn't known better, she would have attributed the flutter in her heart to attraction rather than the excitement of a new case.

Every kidnapping Rachel had investigated since joining the Bureau brought back memories of Caroline, the lifelong friend who'd been like the sister Rachel had never had. Next-door neighbors, they'd grown up together, been roommates in college. After graduation Rachel had gone on to medical school and Caroline had taken a teaching position.

Three months into the fall semester, Rachel had received a call from her mother.

"Mom, what's wrong?" Her heart had accelerated

with fear at the sorrowful tone of her mother's voice. "Dad—"

"Your father's fine. We're all fine." Her mother's voice broke with a sob. "It's Caroline. She's… dead."

"Dead?" The idea was incomprehensible. Her lively friend with the wacky sense of humor and perennial smile couldn't be dead. "What happened?"

"It's too awful to explain over the phone. You'd better come home."

In a fog of disbelief, Rachel drove the thirty miles from the university to Raleigh. There she learned that Caroline had been kidnapped and held for a ransom. Her father, Dr. Kidbrough, a wealthy cardiac surgeon, had paid the ransom, but Caroline wasn't returned. Days later, when her body was found over a hundred miles away on the bank of the Catawba river, the coroner determined Caroline had been killed within hours of her abduction.

Standing over her friend's grave at the funeral service, cold, drizzling rain mixing with her tears, Rachel had vowed to spend her life doing all she could to prevent what had happened to Caroline from happening to others. She never forgot her promise and, upon graduation from medical school, entered the FBI Academy at Quantico, Virginia.

Rachel tried to bring a professional detachment to her work, and she usually succeeded—except in kidnapping cases, where detachment was impossible. She had experienced firsthand the pain and suffering of the victims' families and friends.

She prayed Margaret Maitland was still alive—would stay alive until they could find her.

"What do you think?" she asked Stephen. "Still have that funny feeling about this case?"

He flicked her a quick glance, and in spite of the dim light, his brown eyes gleamed like polished maple. "Something's not right, but I can't put my finger on it."

In the past, Stephen's instincts had proved so accurate, she'd often wondered if he was psychic. "Maitland didn't ask the caller about his wife or insist to speak to her, to assure himself that she's okay. You think the husband might be in on this?"

He shrugged. "Maitland's a strange character. His emotional reactions don't ring true with what I'd expect from a distraught husband, but his behavior could indicate his peculiar personality, not collusion."

"Maybe, but we'd better check out his finances, just the same. See if he's in debt and has an urgent need for a couple million bucks."

Stephen shot her a grin. "That's what I like about you, Doc."

"What?"

"You're so consistently suspicious."

"I am not."

"Then marry me."

"Why?"

With one hand steering expertly, he reached over and ran the warm knuckles of his other across her cheek. "I think I just proved my point."

"Your proof wouldn't hold up in court." She

hoped passing headlights didn't reveal the flush creeping across her face. What was the matter with her, going all soft and gooey inside over a question that was obviously intended as a joke? "Besides, why would you want to ruin a perfectly good friendship by getting married?"

"There you go, being suspicious again."

His tone was teasing, but the momentary heat that had flared in his eyes shocked her. That warmth couldn't have been desire. It must have been a fluke, caused by the lights of oncoming traffic in the twilight.

Curiously shaken, she slid down in her seat. Maybe Stephen was right. Maybe she *was* consistently suspicious. Wariness was appropriate in her line of work, but ever since Brad had broken her heart over four years ago, doubts and uncertainty had ruled her personal life, too.

"I'm not always suspicious." She wondered if her protests were to convince Stephen or herself. "I've trusted you with my life, many times. And I'd do it again. That's what partners are for."

He opened his mouth as if to say something else, but apparently changed his mind. They rode in silence for the next ten minutes.

"Here's the exit." Stephen pulled into the crowded parking area of a brightly lit combination gas station, minimart and stopped the car.

"The pay phone's over there." Rachel pointed to a kiosk on the side of the building where a young woman was making a call. In her arms, a toddler, hands sticky from the candy he held, tried to wrest the receiver from her grasp. "So much for hopes of any fingerprints."

"If we're lucky the clerk will remember something." Stephen slid from the car and headed toward the entrance, and Rachel joined him.

Inside the minimart, a line of people, their arms filled with gallon jugs of milk, loaves of bread and cartons of cigarettes, waited for the harried clerk to ring their purchases. Ignoring the customers' angry glares, Stephen and Rachel moved to the head of the line and showed the clerk their federal identification.

"Great," the plump, gray-haired woman said with a grimace. "First the other cashier calls in sick. Now I've got the FBI to contend with."

"Hurry it up, will ya?" a large man with a beer gut and ruddy face yelled behind them.

Stephen turned to the waiting crowd and raised his gold shield. "This is an official investigation. We won't take long. In the meantime we'd appreciate your cooperation. If anyone's been here longer than twenty minutes, we'd like to talk with you, too."

A few in line murmured among themselves, but the grumbling ceased.

"Did you notice a man using the pay phone outside about twenty minutes ago?" Rachel asked the clerk.

"You've gotta be kidding," the woman said. "It's going-home time, my helper's out sick, and I haven't taken my eyes off the register for the past hour. Someone could have shoplifted half the store, and I wouldn't have seen 'em."

"What about cars?" Stephen said. "A blue—"

"Nope. The president could have gassed up his limousine, and I woulda missed him."

Rachel wasn't about to give up so easily. "Do any of your regular customers drive an old blue Impala? It's a matter of life and death. Think hard, please."

The woman shook her head. "Sorry."

Rachel pulled out her card. "If you remember anything, give me a call."

"What's this all about?" the clerk asked.

"Nothing we can talk about now," Rachel said, "but it *is* urgent. Thanks for your time."

She stepped aside for the impatient customer to place his purchases on the counter.

Stephen eyed the crowd. "Nobody came forward when I asked if anyone had been here over twenty minutes. Looks like we've hit a dead end."

"Maybe not." Rachel nodded toward a preadolescent boy in baggy shorts and T-shirt with a skateboard tucked under his arm, holding a comic at the magazine rack near the exit. "He pretends he's reading, but he hasn't taken his eyes off us since you spoke to the crowd."

"He's worth a try."

As Stephen approached, the boy ducked his head into his book again.

"Been here long?" Stephen asked.

The boy lifted his head and studied them with startled blue eyes, barely visible beneath shaggy blond bangs. "You guys really FBI?"

Stephen flipped open the thin leather folder that held his gold shield with the federal eagle and picture ID and displayed them to the boy.

Wide-eyed, the boy traced the shield with a grubby finger, then glanced at Rachel and back to Stephen. "Wow, just like *The X-Files.*"

"Except we're not after space aliens," Stephen said with a wry smile. "We're looking for a man who used the pay phone here within the last half hour. Did you see him?"

With a panicked look, the boy flung the comic onto the rack, pivoted in his high-topped tennis shoes and headed toward the door. "Gotta go."

"Hold it." Stephen grabbed him by the shoulder. "Just answer my question, son."

The kid jerked from Stephen's grasp. "Leave me alone. I ain't mixed up in this."

"In what?" Rachel asked.

The boy's face blanched, as if he realized he'd said too much. "Whatever you're asking about."

"Even if you could help us save a life?"

The gentleness mixed with urgency in Stephen's voice had its effect. The boy wiped his nose with back of his hand. "He has that man's wife, don't he?"

"How do you know?" Rachel asked.

"I heard him talking. He wants two million dollars to give her back."

Stephen frowned. "Did he know you were listening?"

"Uh-uh. I was around the corner."

"So you didn't see him?"

"No. Didn't want to see him after what I heard."

Rachel's hopes of teaming the boy with a sketch artist evaporated.

"But I saw his car when he drove away. It was a ole beat-up Chevy with a Georgia tag."

"Did you get the number?"

The boy shook his head. "Too far away. But the car headed toward Savannah. Now can I go?"

"Give us your name and address first," Stephen said, "in case we have more questions later."

Rachel jotted the boy's information in her notebook.

"What now?" she asked Stephen when the boy left, swerving through traffic on his skateboard.

"We secure the pay phone and wait for the crime scene technicians. Then we'll go back to the office to start the grunt work."

THE GRUNT WORK made for a long night. The sun was rising over the river marshes when Rachel lifted her head from studying the forensics reports.

Stephen appeared at the door to her office and handed her a cup of freshly brewed coffee. She stretched to ease the knots from her tired muscles and accepted the steaming cup gratefully.

"Any luck?" he asked.

"No prints on Maitland's car and no tire tracks at the abduction scene. The pay phone and kiosk at the minimart yielded hundreds of prints, but the most promising are a few partials lifted from quarters at the top of the coin box."

"Quarters left by the most recent callers?"

She nodded. "I'm running them through the Automated Fingerprint Identification System. AFIS should have some names for us within the hour."

Stephen rubbed his eyes with his fists, reminding her of a sleepy little boy and evoking a tenderness that took her by surprise.

She sipped the coffee and lowered her eyes to hide her unexpected emotion. "Did you find anything on Maitland?"

"His credit rating is excellent." He stifled a yawn. "I'm still accessing his accounts. But if he's engaged in anything shady, like gambling debts to the mob, it won't show up on his bank records."

"So there's nothing so far to incriminate him?"

"Except Margaret Maitland's will. Her father was more than happy to fill me in on the particulars. He hates his son-in-law with a passion."

Rachel's heart sank. "Harold Maitland is Margaret's beneficiary?"

Grim-faced, Stephen nodded. "And Margaret, thanks to an enormous trust fund from her grandfather, is a very wealthy woman."

The pain of Caroline's death, which had blunted over time, returned with piercing intensity, multiplying Rachel's fears for Margaret's safety. "What do your instincts tell you? Is Margaret still alive?"

Before Stephen could answer, the phone on Rachel's desk chimed. She glanced at the flashing indicator. "It's your line."

Stephen punched the button and grabbed the receiver. "Agent Chandler."

His expression registered surprise, but he said nothing more, listening for a few minutes, before reaching for pencil and paper, and writing quickly.

"We're on our way," he said.

"They found her?" Rachel asked when he hung up.

"No, but the sheriff's office had a tip."

She closed the forensics folder and pushed away from her desk. She hadn't slept in twenty-four hours, and her stomach was empty, but all thoughts of food and sleep vanished at Stephen's alert expression. "What kind of tip?"

"A farmer north of town heard noises and saw lights in the woods near his house an hour before dawn."

"How does that relate to Margaret Maitland?"

"The farmer heard voices, two men and a woman's. By the time he got dressed and went out with his dog to check on his property, the people had vanished in an old Chevy barreling past his house."

Rachel shivered. If the men had been the kidnappers and the woman Margaret Maitland, any one of several explanations existed for their presence in the woods, none of them good.

"We'd better hurry," she said.

Stephen was already headed for the door. "A deputy will join us at the farm with a tracking dog. We'll swing by the Maitland house on the way and pick up something with Margaret's scent."

AN HOUR LATER, Rachel, Stephen and two deputies were tramping through a pine forest thick with underbrush and pine needles and hastening to keep up with the bloodhound who had picked up a scent almost immediately from the Hermes scarf Harold Maitland had provided. He and Parker Dayvault had demanded to participate in the search, but Jason, who had remained at the house to ask more questions and monitor the phones, insisted they were needed to answer the phones in case the kidnappers called again. Reluctantly the husband and father had agreed to stay behind.

It was just as well. Rachel had no idea whether the bloodhound would lead them to the place the abductors had hidden Margaret...or to her body. Her heart sank when the search party broke into a small clearing centered with a mound of freshly turned dirt.

"We're too late." She blinked back tears.

The bloodhound began digging furiously at the fresh earth.

"Get shovels from the farmhouse," Stephen ordered the other deputy, who took off at a run.

Stephen dropped to his knees and began digging with his hands. Rachel and the other deputy joined him, but without tools, progress was slow. The bloodhound continued his frantic pawing, scattering dirt across the clearing and into Rachel's eyes.

After a few minutes that seemed like hours, the deputy returned, bringing two men and several shovels. For the next ten minutes, nothing sounded in the clearing except the *ker-chunk* of shovels slicing through the earth and the rain of dirt onto piles that steadily grew.

Rachel stood to the side with the deputy who restrained the dog, while Stephen, the other deputy and the farmer and his son attacked the earth. Stephen had removed his coat and tie and rolled the sleeves of his dress shirt. In the humid summer air, the imported cotton, wet with sweat, delineated the firm muscles of his back and chest and the power of his movements. His generous mouth, set in a hard, thin line, showed his determination.

Emotions ambushed Rachel again, and admiration and a strange tenderness flooded her as she watched Stephen work. If she were ever in trouble, she hoped she'd have a champion like him to rush to her aid. Lack of sleep was making her punchy. She shook her head to dispel the sentimental thoughts.

Suddenly the thud of metal on wood reverberated through the woods. With the shovel's blade, Stephen scraped earth from broad pine planks.

"It's a casket," the farmer said. "You boys might as well slow down and rest. If somebody's in there, she ain't going nowhere."

"No," Stephen yelled and increased the pace of his shoveling. "Keep digging!"

Fearing the farmer was right, Rachel was afraid to hope, but the men followed Stephen's order. Within a few minutes, they had stripped the dirt from the lid of the pine box.

The farmer pointed to its edges. "I told you whoever's in there is a goner. It's nailed tighter than a miser's fist."

Ignoring the wizened old man, Stephen forced the blade of his shovel beneath the casket lid and pried. The deputy, following Stephen's lead, did the same on the other side. With the screech of yielding nails, the lid broke free and they tossed it aside.

Rachel's breath caught in her throat. Inside the makeshift coffin lay the body of Margaret Maitland, her golden hair tousled, her clothes shredded, and worst of all, the nails of her hands bloodied where she had tried to scratch her way out of the pine box.

"The bastards." A sound like a sob caught in Stephen's throat. "They buried her alive."

Rachel pushed him aside and laid her hand against Margaret's neck. A pulse, weak but steady, fluttered beneath her fingers. "She's alive! Get her out of here. She needs a doctor."

With a compassion that brought tears to Rachel's eyes, Stephen gathered the unconscious woman in his arms and, with the deputies' help, climbed from the hole and started back toward the highway. While one deputy raced ahead to call an ambulance, the other deputy helped Rachel secure the crime scene—or what little evidence was left after their frantic excavation.

AFTER A SHOWER and change of clothes, Rachel and Stephen visited Margaret Maitland at the hospital later that morning. The private room, guarded in the hall by a Savannah cop, was crowded with her husband and parents and the FBI sketch artist.

Margaret, conscious now and propped against her pillows with a flush of color in her cheeks, smiled at the new arrivals from her bed. The only visible sign of her ordeal was her bandaged hands.

Serena Dayvault, her aged, aristocratic face glowing with gratitude, swept toward Rachel and Stephen like a queen at a reception. "You saved my daughter. I can't thank you enough."

Parker Dayvault unashamedly wiped tears with a

monogrammed handkerchief. Harold Maitland, standing stoically beside Margaret's pillow, hands clasped behind his back, showed only the effects of a bad hangover.

"I'm sorry," Stephen said, "but you must all leave so we can question Mrs. Maitland."

Dayvault drew himself to full height. "Now see here—"

"Be quiet, Parker," his wife said softly, but the effect was the same as if she'd shouted. "These people have a job to do and we're in the way. We'll come back later, sweetheart," she said to Margaret.

Parker followed his wife meekly out of the room. Harold kissed his wife on the forehead and, avoiding the agents' eyes, left without a word.

"We're almost finished, anyway." The sketch artist set aside her pad. "I'll take a coffee break."

Stephen stepped to the bedside. "Do you feel strong enough to answer a few questions?"

Margaret nodded, offered him a weak smile, and self-consciously adjusted the neckline of her hospital gown. Rachel suppressed a smile of her own. She had yet to run into a woman who didn't respond to Stephen. His unpretentious sincerity, combined with his compelling good looks, usually had women falling all over themselves to answer his questions.

Rachel pulled a chair beside the bed. "The doctor says you're going to be fine."

"A bump on the head and broken fingernails seem minor when, except for the FBI, I'd be dead." Margaret shivered, as if remembering.

"Our work isn't over," Stephen said. "Not until

the men who did this to you are behind bars. Had you ever seen them before?''

Margaret shook her head. "Never."

"Where did they take you," he asked, "after they pulled you from your car?"

"I couldn't see." Margaret's soft drawl had the cadence of her mother's but was more hesitant than the steel magnolia's tone. "They blindfolded me, tied my hands and feet, and laid me on the back seat. They didn't remove the blindfold until they took me to the woods."

Stephen placed his hand gently across her bandaged, shaking ones. "I know answering is hard, but we have to find these men before they harm someone else."

Margaret brightened at his touch. "I understand."

Stephen returned her smile. "Did these men ever give any indication they weren't working alone?"

"I only heard the two of them."

"They never contacted or referred to anyone else, someone they might have been working for?"

Margaret frowned. "They mentioned several times that if they didn't follow the plan, they wouldn't get paid. But I thought they were referring to the ransom."

"Did they call each other by name?" Rachel asked.

Margaret nodded. "The tall man was Bubba. He called the short one Weed. That's not much help, is it?"

"The nicknames may pop up in our computer files," Rachel said.

She removed a folder from her briefcase. When AFIS had identified fingerprints from the pay phone coins, two of the hits had criminal records with mug shots on file. She had mixed the photos of the two suspects with a half dozen other mug shots. After pulling a rolling table across the bed, she spread the pictures for Margaret to study. "Do any of these men look familiar?"

The woman's gaze flitted over the first few shots without recognition. Then she gasped. "That's him! That's Bubba."

"You're certain?" Stephen asked.

"Absolutely." Margaret shuddered. "That ugly face will haunt me the rest of my life."

"You're safe now," Rachel assured her. "It's only a matter of time until we catch Bubba and his pal."

Later, in the hospital elevator, empty except for the two of them, Stephen turned to Rachel. "Melvin Tucker, alias Bubba, is just a two-bit crook. I find it hard to believe he and this Weed planned the kidnapping alone."

"You think they were working for someone else?"

"We'll know when we bring them in" he said. "No doubt, we offer them a deal and they'll spill their guts."

BUBBA AND WEED never had a chance to reveal whether someone else had hired them. That afternoon, acting on a call to a tip line, Agent Jason Bender had stormed the room the kidnappers had rented in a seedy hotel. When they drew weapons, Jason shot and killed them both.

The capture had been a coup for Jason, who'd often failed to hide his resentment at working in Stephen's shadow. Local media proclaimed him a hero, and the Dayvaults presented him with a hefty check as a reward. If Jason hadn't risked his own life in storming the room where the kidnappers had holed up, Rachel would have found his cockiness less tolerable. Another event turned her attention from Jason's boastfulness.

Two days after the shootings, Stephen was promoted to the Atlanta office. The Maitland kidnapping was the last case he and Rachel worked as partners. What happened afterward had nothing to do with the FBI.

Chapter Three

Where was Stephen?

Rachel paced the broad front porch of Stephen's mountain safe house and peered into the midnight darkness. Far below, barely visible through the trees, the headlights of an occasional passing car stabbed the blackness on the highway, but none turned up the winding mountain road.

Stephen's warning had come ten hours ago, and there was still no sign of him. If he had called from Atlanta, he'd been less than four hours away.

What was taking him so long?

She shuddered at the possibility that some unknown person whose threat Stephen had uncovered might have caught up with him, but she immediately dismissed those fears.

Not Stephen.

He was too smart. Too careful.

Too dear.

Drawing her jacket closer around her, she sank onto the stairs, glad for the reassuring bulk of her automatic pistol in her shoulder holster. Stephen had selected a safe house in the middle of nowhere, miles from its nearest neighbor, even farther from the closest town. Her only contact with civilization was the telephone, but she didn't dare call anyone. Not before Stephen could explain the danger that stalked them. Depending on the level of sophistication—and desperation—of the people who sought to harm her— they might have tapped her home and office phones and that of her parents in Raleigh in an attempt to trace her.

There was nothing to do but wait. And pray that Stephen was okay.

She hadn't seen him in sixteen months, hadn't had the courage to face him, even to speak with him, after their last disastrous encounter. She never would have guessed a simple going-away party could have caused such fateful and unexpected consequences.

The party had started out simply enough. She and Jason Bender had organized the surprise celebration at Stephen's apartment. Because Rachel had a key Stephen had given her so she could water his plants whenever he was out of town, and Jason had cornered Stephen for the day with a request for assistance on a bank fraud case he was working, the secret preparations had been a breeze.

She had met the caterers at the apartment and hung balloons, a good-luck banner and streamers. Later she directed guests to hide their cars so Stephen wouldn't see them when he arrived. Somehow almost fifty people—everyone in the Savannah FBI office, local law enforcement personnel, federal and district attorneys, and several of Stephen's neighbors—had crowded into his small place.

His reaction when he'd unlocked his door and stepped inside was something she would never forget. Luckily she had anticipated it, or he might have accidentally shot someone when he went for his gun.

Her own reflexes as quick as his, she had flung her arms around his neck, effectively blocking his ability to draw. At that point, her innate reticence evaporated. Without a thought for the consequences, she had pressed her lips to his mouth and kissed him, while all around them, fifty voices shouted, "Surprise!"

The other guests might as well have been on another planet. Oblivious of her audience, she yielded to the warmth of Stephen's embrace, the exhilarating taste of him, the thrum of his pulse beneath her fingers caressing his neck.

He pulled back first, and his dark eyes burned into hers. "Well, that *was* a surprise."

She covered her indiscretion quickly. "Diversionary tactic only, Chandler. Couldn't have you shooting your own guests. The Bureau wouldn't like it. And it would tend to lower your social rating, too."

"On a scale of one to ten," he said, "I'd rate that diversion a fifteen."

"Just another of my hidden talents."

"You have others?"

"Hundreds."

"I'm impressed."

"Too bad. Now that you're moving to Atlanta, you'll never know them."

His arms tightened around her. "If they're as outstanding as that kiss, maybe I should turn down that promotion and hang around.''

His searing look took her breath away and robbed her of further words. She was saved by guests surging around them, clapping Stephen on the back with congratulations on his promotion. He released her, and she faded into the crowd. With Stephen preoccupied, she slipped away to the kitchen to splash cold water on her overheated face.

She had no idea what had come over her. She was acting like a lovestruck teenager—and Stephen was her best friend, for Pete's sake, not her lover.

She dried her face, picked up a tray of glasses and returned to the living room, where Jason and another agent, Stan Lewolsky, were opening bottles of champagne. Avoiding Stephen's gaze, she wandered among the guests, making small talk. His questioning glance followed her around the room like a heat-seeking missile.

An apt analogy, she thought ironically, since her cheeks flamed every time she remembered his kiss.

In an attempt to soothe her inner turmoil, she—who rarely touched alcohol of any kind—downed glass after glass of champagne, until the sounds and activity of the party swirled around her in an ever-increasing blur.

The bubbly had gone straight to her head. She'd started imagining things, like the sultry looks of longing that Stephen cast her way, and the strange expression, almost of loathing, that she'd caught from Jason Bender. He'd probably been appalled by her uncharacteristic behavior.

A flicker of light in the mountain valley jerked her back to the present, and her pulse went into overdrive. Already shivering from the cold, she trembled harder, wondering if the vehicle making its slow, steady climb up the mountain was Stephen or his unnamed assailants.

Considering the possibility they might have found Stephen and forced him to reveal where she was, she stepped into the shadow of the porch. She kept telling herself it had to be Stephen but she withdrew her gun from its holster just the same.

She lost sight momentarily of the lights on the road below, but she could hear the crunch of tires on gravel and the engine straining in low gear as it climbed the steep incline toward the cabin. She flattened herself out of sight around the corner just as the car's headlights swept the clearing in front of the house.

The vehicle parked next to her Explorer, and its engine stopped. Having seen her sport utility vehicle, whoever was driving would know she was here. Gun ready, she held her breath and waited.

No one emerged from the dark car.

Her nerves stretched taut, Rachel didn't move. The only sounds were the wind soughing through the trees, the rustle of a small creature scuttling through dry leaves, and the distant, plaintive hoot of an owl.

Remembering her tactical training from her academy days at Quantico, Rachel sidled around to the back of the cabin and slipped into the woods. With her ears attuned to any noise from the car or its occupants, she picked her way through the trees, placing her feet carefully to avoid tipping off her presence.

In spite of the cold, she broke into a sweat from a healthy dose of fear and the effort of moving stealthily.

After minutes that seemed like agonizing hours, she had positioned herself in the cover of trees a few feet from the strange car.

Moonlight flooded the clearing in front of the cabin, illuminating the dark Taurus, typical of a government-issued vehicle. But if the car was Stephen's, why hadn't he exited to let her know he'd arrived?

The fact that no one had gotten out aroused Rachel's suspicions. And accelerated her fears. Was this the danger Stephen had warned her about? Had someone found him? And if so, was Stephen harmed...or worse?

Rachel pressed the heel of her hand against her lips to suppress a moan. Swift, hot anger quickly dispersed the pain, stiffening her resolve. If they had harmed Stephen, she'd make certain they paid.

At the click of a door latch, she focused on the vehicle and lifted her automatic to the ready. Whoever this was, he wouldn't enter the cabin without going through her first.

The driver's door swung open.

The dome light flicked on and illuminated the interior and the driver slumped across the wheel, not moving. She couldn't see his face, couldn't tell anything about him except that he wore a suit jacket and had dark hair.

Aware of the likelihood of a trap, Rachel maneuvered through the trees at the edge of the clearing until she could view the lit back seat.

Empty.

The driver couldn't have opened the door in his sleep. What was going on?

There was only one way to find out.

Gun braced before her, she raced silently across the clearing to the open door, and shoved the barrel against the driver's temple.

"Put your hands on the wheel," she yelled.

The driver groaned and turned his head. Deathly pale, Stephen stared up at her.

"Thank God, you made it, Doc." His voice was barely a whisper.

Rachel shoved her gun in her holster and reached for him, but when her hand clasped his arm, she drew back. Her fingers were sticky with blood.

"Are you all right?" she asked. "What happened?"

"Shot," he murmured, "but he didn't follow me. I lost him outside Atlanta."

She cast an uneasy glance down the mountain toward the dark highway. "You're sure?"

"I wasn't followed."

She had to get him inside before he went into shock—if he wasn't in that state already. "Can you walk?"

"I'll try."

She knelt beside the seat, swung his legs out, lifted his uninjured arm over her shoulder and tugged him from the car. He stumbled against her, and they almost fell, but she managed to stay upright.

"It isn't far," she said. "Just rest your weight on me and move your feet."

Straining to support him, she shuffled toward the porch, then half carried, half dragged him up the stairs and into the cabin's main room. She lowered him onto the overstuffed sofa, and eased him onto his back.

"I have to get this jacket off you, see how much blood you've lost."

"Good thing you're a doctor, eh, Doc?" He smiled weakly.

"Wait'll you get my bill, then see if you're still smiling," she said in a feeble attempt at humor.

His expression transformed to a grimace of pain when she lifted him and stripped off his jacket. Her knees threatened to buckle at the sight of his blood-drenched shirt, and her heart fluttered in panic.

She wasn't a practicing doctor. She had completed medical school but none of her internship. From the looks of all that blood, Stephen needed someone experienced in treating gunshot trauma.

Tamping down her rising anxiety, she rummaged through a desk on the opposite side of the room and found a pair of scissors. After removing his Glock semiautomatic and shoulder holster with quivering fingers, she slid off his tie and cut away the blood-stained shirt.

"Is there a first aid kit in this place?" she asked.

"Over the kitchen sink," he muttered through chattering teeth.

She covered his bare chest with an afghan, threw more logs on the fire, and went in search of medical supplies. A few minutes later she returned with the kit, a basin of warm water and an armful of towels.

After she had cleaned and bandaged his arm, her

apprehension diminished somewhat. The bullet had passed clean through the flesh and muscle, miraculously missing bones and major arteries, but he had lost a great deal of blood.

"We should get you to a hospital," she said.

"You know that…doctors are required to report gunshot wounds," he said in a voice growing fainter with each word. "We can't take…the chance of tipping…him off to our location."

"Who? Who's after us?"

"Later… Safe now." His eyelids sagged. "Too tired…"

He grew so still, her fears resurged with a vengeance, but when she checked his pulse, its steadiness reassured her. She tossed his ruined shirt into the fire and carried the basin and first aid kit back to the kitchen.

A hasty search of the main bedroom turned up a man's flannel shirt in a closet. Gently she put it on him and buttoned it against the cold. He didn't awaken, not even when she plumped thick pillows behind his head and added a handmade quilt over the afghan.

One thing was certain. Until she knew the exact nature of the threat—who was after them and why— she wouldn't relax her guard. She checked her patient again, then went into the kitchen long enough to brew a pot of strong coffee. It was going to be a long night.

Later, curled in a deep chair beside the sofa, her hands warmed by a mug of hot coffee, she studied Stephen as he slept. He hadn't changed. His hair was cropped a bit shorter, in the conservative style male agents were encouraged to adhere to, but otherwise, he looked the same.

Square, determined jaw.

High, sculpted cheekbones and broad, intelligent forehead.

Thick dark eyelashes any woman would kill for.

But there was nothing effeminate about Stephen Chandler. Even in repose, his rugged strength was evident, despite his pallor from loss of blood.

The last time she'd watched him sleeping had been the morning after his going-away party. If it hadn't been for too much champagne...

In spite of the success of the party and the intensity of the revelry, she had been stricken with a mind-numbing sadness. Until that night, she hadn't really grasped the fact that Stephen would no longer be a fixture in her life. She wouldn't wake up every morning knowing that the next eight to twelve hours, and often more, would be spent in the pleasure of his company. Days, weeks, months without Stephen had stretched before her like a deep, yawning abyss.

Figuring the champagne was making her maudlin, she shook her head, trying to dispel her gloomy thoughts. After all, he was only a friend—a great friend, but just a buddy, nonetheless. And she had plenty of other friends to fill the gap when Stephen left the following day.

When all the guests departed, she had stayed behind to wash glasses and clean up from the party so his apartment would be ready for the movers when they came to pack the next day. After the last goodbye, Stephen had discovered her weeping into the dishwater.

"Hey, Doc, great party."

"I'm glad you enjoyed it," she said with an audible sniff.

"You okay?"

She had hastily wiped away her tears, leaving a trail of soapsuds across her cheeks. "I should never drink champagne. It makes me weepy every time," she lied.

With a tenderness that only increased her sadness, he drew her into his arms and cleaned the suds from her cheeks with gentle fingers. "Are you sure it's the bubbly making you teary?"

"Don't be silly. What else would it be?"

"Aren't you just a little bit sad I'm leaving?"

His warm breath caressed her face, and she had to fight the urge to meld her body against his.

"Of course I'm sad," she admitted. "You're the best partner I've ever had."

"You could come with me."

"*I* didn't get a promotion."

He ran his fingers along the line of her jaw, sending shivers of pleasure racing across her skin. "You could request a transfer."

"The Bureau might frown on that."

"Then hang the Bureau and marry me."

"Be serious."

"What makes you think I'm not?" His eyes gleamed with a fierce light in the dim kitchen.

"Because you've asked me a dozen times before, and you've never been serious."

"Doc—"

"We're friends, Stephen. That's all."

His proximity was making breathing difficult. She attempted to wriggle from his arms, but he held her fast.

"I have to finish washing—"

His lips cut off her words, and she yielded to the warmth of his kiss before her befuddled brain sent her paralyzed muscles into action. She pushed away and plunged her hands back into the tepid dishwater, but Stephen wasn't deterred.

He moved behind her, wrapped his arms around her waist, and pulled her against the hard, taut muscles of his torso. "Stop fighting this. I know you feel something for me."

"All I feel," she said breathlessly, hoping by taking the offensive to protect herself from her own dangerous impulses, "is that uncomfortable bulge in your jeans. Admit it, you've had too much to drink. You're not thinking with your head."

He whipped her around to face him, apparently oblivious of her dripping hands against his shirt, and drew her close, so close she could feel the pounding of his heart.

Or was that her own?

"You'd feel it, too, Doc, if you'd break through that damned wall you've built around yourself. Get over it. Brad was almost five years ago. This is now."

"You're not being fair."

He cocked a finger beneath her chin and tilted her head until she was gazing straight into his eyes. "What's not fair is your wasting the rest of your life because some creep didn't know a prize when he had her.''

His words stunned her. ''You think I'm a prize?''

''Haven't I always said so?''

He had her dazed, confused, overcome with emotions so alien, she couldn't tell if they were real. She raised anger as a shield. ''I'm not some trophy, a notch you can add to your belt of conquests—''

''From the first day you walked into the Savannah office, I've been crazy about you.''

''You're crazy, all right.'' She shook her head. ''You've had too much to drink, and you're confusing things.''

''Things?''

''Confusing me.''

''I know what I'm saying. I don't want to go to Atlanta without you.''

He kissed her again, slowly, gently. The taste of him ignited a fire in her blood, and before she could stop herself, she was opening her lips to him and wrapping her arms around his neck.

The heat of his kiss burned away the last of her inhibitions, and when he lifted her in his arms and carried her toward the bedroom, she didn't protest.

The rest of the night passed like a dream, hazy images she wasn't sure she could trust when she awakened the next morning at dawn. Had Stephen really shattered her self-imposed reserve, swept her to the heights of passion she'd never known, vowed his love for her?

She glanced at him, sleeping naked beside her, his

magnificent body half-covered by a sheet, one tanned, muscled arm draped across her bare breasts.

Stephen, her best friend.

Stephen, *her lover?*

She bit her lips to suppress a moan of dismay. She'd acted like a fool, weeping like a child, all but throwing herself into his arms. Embarrassment wiped away the flush of sated contentment she'd experienced at awakening in his arms. With her recklessness and lack of control, she had effectively destroyed the best friendship she'd ever had.

Moving quietly not to awaken him, she tugged on her clothes, but she hadn't been able to resist one last kiss before she slipped out the door. At the fleeting touch of her lips, he had smiled and reached for her in his sleep.

For the rest of the weekend she had refused to answer her telephone. He probably wanted to apologize for letting the champagne go to his head, just as she had. But she couldn't face him. He must have thought she'd lost her mind. Each time she weakened and reached for the ringing phone, she recalled the intensity of their lovemaking, the fool she'd made of herself, and didn't answer. She spent hours driving aimlessly in case he showed up at her door.

On Monday, Jason Bender told her Stephen had stopped by the office before leaving for Atlanta, but Rachel was out interviewing a manager whose bank had been robbed. By the following Monday, she'd managed to avoid all Stephen's calls to the office, and her home phone had finally stopped its incessant ringing.

By that time, Rachel had admitted to herself the real reason for her avoidance of Stephen. She was afraid she was falling in love with him, and the prospect terrified her. She wouldn't endure again the heartache and humiliation Brad had put her through when he'd ended their engagement. Better to remain unattached with her lonely heart in one piece than risk such pain again.

But missing Stephen brought its special kind of pain.

The passing weeks, however, justified her reservations. Through the office grapevine, three months after his move, she learned Stephen had formed a serious relationship with an Atlanta advertising executive, Anne Michelle Logan, a former Miss University of Georgia.

Along with that news came rumors of an impending marriage.

This information arrived the same day her doctor confirmed what those little drugstore test kits had been telling her for weeks, but she'd refused to believe until now.

She was pregnant with Stephen's child.

Determined that Stephen not know, she had resigned from the Bureau and taken the forensics job with the sheriff's department in North Carolina, far enough from Atlanta not to run into Stephen by accident, and far enough from Savannah that her former colleagues wouldn't guess what had happened or pass the news to Stephen.

She hadn't wanted to upset the plans for his upcoming marriage. He was so damned *honorable,* had he learned of her pregnancy, he would have insisted on marrying her. Marriage to Stephen was the last thing she wanted. His falling in love so quickly after reaching Atlanta proved her point that they had been friends only. Since he'd found a woman he loved, Rachel refused to saddle him with her and her child for the rest of his life.

After cutting herself off from former friends, she had been horribly lonely.

Until Jessica was born.

Her beautiful daughter, with dark hair and eyes like her father's had filled her life with laughter and love. Soon Rachel had made new friends at her new job. Everything had seemed to be working out all right.

Then came Stephen's call, warning her of danger.

He had warned her not to stop for anything on her way to the mountains, but Rachel had stopped at the day care center to pick up Jessica, then stopped again at a grocery in Sylva to buy formula and disposable diapers. Jessica slept now in the next room.

With Stephen sleeping soundly on the sofa, she set aside her empty coffee mug, shoved to her feet and tiptoed to the smaller bedroom to check on her daughter, snuggled happily between bolsters of pillows that kept her from rolling off the wide double bed.

By the dim glow of a nightlight, Rachel could see Jessica clearly, a tiny smile dimpling her plump cheeks as she slept. She was such a good baby and so adaptable, the long ride and arrival at a strange place hadn't fazed her in the least. She had eaten her supper with her usual relish and gone straight to sleep.

Rachel's heart wrenched at the dilemma before her.

Would Stephen recognize himself in his daughter? Could Rachel manage to shave a few months off Jessica's age without rousing his suspicions?

Her long months of solitude and sacrifice would come to nothing if Stephen were to learn Jessica was *his* daughter. He had probably married his Georgia beauty queen by now. Rachel didn't want herself or her daughter to become the object of his embarrassment or his pity. She would lie if she had to. For all their sakes.

She had leaned over the pillows to kiss her daughter, to revel in her sweet baby scent, when an explosion of noise in the living room jerked her upright. Jessica stirred and whimpered at the sound, but continued sleeping. Afraid the person who had shot Stephen had caught up with them, Rachel switched off the night-light and drew her gun. Covered by darkness, she shifted silently to the open door and gazed into the living room.

Illuminated only by the flickering light of the dying fire, the room danced with shadows. The front door remained closed, the deadbolt locked, but the sofa where Stephen had slept was empty.

Determined to protect her daughter at all costs, Rachel stepped into the living room and drew the bedroom door closed behind her.

When she spotted Stephen, sprawled across the oval braided rug in front of the fireplace with his head resting on the raised stone hearth, she stifled a cry of dismay.

But she couldn't go to him. Not yet.

A quick search of the house convinced her there

had been no intruder, and she returned to the living room. Stephen must have attempted to stand and passed out. Holstering her gun, she grabbed him beneath his arms and dragged him back to the sofa.

When she had settled him against the pillows, checked his wound and covered him against the cold, she discovered the large knot on his temple. He had cracked his head against the stone hearth when he fainted.

She went into the kitchen, returned with a basin of cool water and began to bathe his face. She had to bring him back to consciousness and force him to name the person who threatened them. Without knowing who he was, she couldn't arrange for Jessica's safety, and it was too dangerous to keep her daughter with her when a killer was apparently on her trail.

Stephen moaned beneath her care but didn't open his eyes. Frustrated, she gave up on reviving him with cold water and threw more logs on the fire.

Outside, the wind picked up, shaking the trees, scraping branches across the roof and swirling leaves against the windows. The gravity of her position weighed on her. An unconscious man and a helpless infant, both relying on her to keep them safe.

But safe from *whom?* Only Stephen knew, and he wasn't talking, at least not anytime soon.

She eyed the telephone longingly across the room. One quick call to her parents in Raleigh, and they could be here in a few hours to take Jessica to safety. But, depending on the determination and capabilities of the person who sought them, one call could also alert her enemy to her exact location.

She went into the kitchen, refilled her mug with coffee and returned to the living room to pace the braided rug before the fireplace. Stephen had said only that the threats involved a case they had worked together in Savannah. But over a span of four years they had worked hundreds of cases, too long ago to remember every detail but too soon for any of the criminals they had put away to have been released from jail.

Could someone they'd arrested and successfully prosecuted have escaped, set on vengeance? Or maybe been released after winning an appeal? Her self-imposed exile had cut her off not only from her friends in the Bureau but from all knowledge related to her former cases, as well.

"Wake up, Stephen," she muttered. "*Please* wake up."

As if responding to her plea, he stirred on the sofa and groaned.

Rachel slammed her cup onto the mantel and rushed to his side. "Stephen, can you hear me?"

His thick lashes fluttered. He lifted a hand to the knot on his forehead and winced when he touched it.

"What happened?" he asked.

"You tried to get up and fell and hit your head."

He opened his eyes and stared at her. A look of confusion took over his features. "Who are you?"

"I'm Rachel."

"Where am I?"

She clasped his hands in hers. His temporary disorientation was understandable after all he'd been through—a gunshot wound, loss of blood, a blow to the head—but he had to order his thoughts so he could tell her who was after them.

"You're at the safe house in the mountains."

"Safe house?" His broad forehead wrinkled, as if struggling to recall.

"You remember, don't you, Stephen?"

"Stephen?" His dark eyes widened and stared into hers. "Is that my name?"

The implication of his question drove the air from her lungs. "You're Stephen Chandler."

He squinted at her with dazed eyes. "If you say so."

"Don't you remember?"

He gaped at her as if she were crazy. "Sorry, but I don't seem to remember anything."

Chapter Four

He felt as if he'd been hit by a speeding truck. His left arm ached, his head pounded and his efforts at concentration accelerated the pain. Lying back against the pillows, he closed his eyes.

"Don't!" Her cry startled him, just as he was about to doze off.

Rachel. That's what she'd said her name was.

She settled on the sofa beside him, and he was inundated by the familiar perfume of roses and an unnamed longing. From a distance she looked like a beautiful dream; up close she was even prettier. He could see smooth, flawless skin with an apricot glow along high cheekbones, lustrous blond hair that tumbled over her shoulders and shining eyes the color of spring leaves. Concern wrinkled the perfection of her forehead, and he resisted the impulse to smooth the worried crease with his fingers. With reluctance he dropped his scrutiny and returned his attention to her peculiar warning.

"'Don't,' you said. Don't what?"

"Don't go to sleep. You've fallen and banged your

head, and you could have a concussion. If you sleep, you could lapse into a coma.''

She switched on the lamp on the end table, and he blinked in its glare. With gentle fingers, she pried open his lids and peered purposefully into his eyes.

''You a doctor?'' he asked.

''I'm familiar enough with head trauma to know you'd better stay awake for a while.''

Since he'd come to a few moments ago, two predominant emotions had warred within him. One, an overwhelming sense of urgency and impending danger, and the other, an irresistible affinity for the woman who'd filled his vision when he first opened his eyes.

''Are you my wife?''

Her pained expression answered before her words. ''No, I'm not your wife.''

''But I know you?''

''I'm Rachel Goforth. We were partners for four years.''

He shook his head, which did nothing to clear his confusion and only increased the throbbing at his temples. ''What kind of partners?''

She smoothed his pillow and tucked an afghan over his chest. ''Would you like some coffee? It'll help you stay awake.''

''I want answers.''

''No reason you can't have both.'' Her smile was warm but he could read the worry in her eyes. ''I'll be right back.''

He watched her cross the room and enter the kitchen, separated from the living area only by a peninsula. Petite and slender, she wore camel-colored slacks and a matching pullover that emphasized her slim hips and the swell of her small breasts as she reached into an overhead cupboard for a mug.

Her movement also called attention to the weapon she carried in a shoulder holster, an incongruous accessory for a beautiful woman. Considering his injuries, he wondered if he was her prisoner, but the idea didn't sit right. Instinct assured him this woman wasn't a threat. There had to be another explanation.

He'd think of it if his head stopped pounding.

She filled a mug with coffee and added two sugars before returning to the living room and handing it to him, along with two white caplets.

"What's this?" he asked.

"Acetaminophen, for pain."

He ached, as much from confusion as the bump on his head. He'd suffered a blow to his temple and some kind of injury to his arm. Someone was obviously out to harm him, but for the life of him, he felt no menace from the woman who sank into the large chair beside the sofa and studied him with anxious eyes. He swallowed the pills with a sip of coffee, but his stomach rebelled at the hot acidic liquid, and he set the mug aside.

"What kind of partners were we?" he repeated.

"FBI. We worked four years in the Savannah office."

He glanced past her to a jacket, hung over the back of a straight chair. The patch on the sleeve read, "Cleveland County, N.C., Sheriff's Office."

"That yours?"

She nodded. "I left the Bureau over a year ago."

"Why?"

Her eyelids fluttered, as if she were thinking fast. "I wanted to settle down, have a family. Tough to do, the way the Bureau relocates its agents regularly."

"And this place?" He waved his uninjured arm, indicating the rustic cabin's interior. "Is it yours?"

She shook her head. "You called me yesterday and asked me to meet you here..."

She filled him in on the details. Apparently he had learned of a threat to their lives from someone connected to a case he and Rachel had worked together in Savannah. He had warned her and told her to meet him in the mountains where they would both be safe while he brought her up to speed on what was happening.

Evidently the threat was real, as evidenced by the bullet hole in his left arm. Unfortunately, with his memory gone, they had no clue as to who was after them or why.

If she was telling the truth.

"How do I know *you* didn't shoot me?" Instinct continued to insist she was no threat, but it also prompted him to ask, to gauge her reaction.

"You don't." She pulled her semiautomatic from its holster, removed the clip and showed him the ammunition loaded there. "But if I'd hit you with one of these bullets, there wouldn't be much left of your upper arm. From the small, clean hole, I'd say you were shot with a small caliber, probably a .22."

"The close-range hit man's weapon of choice."

"You remember." Her amazing green eyes lit with hope.

"Sorry." He shook his head until the pain stopped him short, "Don't know how I remember that. But I still don't recall anything about myself."

She peered at him with a worried frown. "I should take you to the emergency room and have your head and arm checked out."

"Too risky, since we don't know who's after us or how close they may be."

"We can't just sit here, waiting for whoever it is to find us."

He wanted to close his eyes and sleep for a week, forget that a nameless, faceless killer was on his trail. The only thing that made consciousness bearable was the presence of the woman who shared his exile. Maybe he couldn't remember her, but the tenderness she evoked made him believe she'd been more than simply a former partner. An overpowering protectiveness flooded him, accompanied by an equal dose of frustration at his lack of memory.

"Rachel…"

"Yes?"

"Were we…close?"

An appealing blush appeared at her hairline and flooded to her neck at the crisp white collar that peeked above her sweater. With slender fingers she combed a strand of hair off her forehead and avoided his gaze by staring at the fire.

"We were…good friends," she finally said. "Like…brother and sister. But we…lost touch after you moved to Atlanta."

The crack on his head hadn't damaged his instincts. For the first time, he had the distinct impression she wasn't telling the truth. But why would she lie about the past? According to her account, they had been traveling separate paths for a long time now.

Trying to unravel the contradictions between her words and his instincts exhausted him. "You're not going to let me sleep?" he asked.

She shook her head, and again he caught the familiar scent of roses. "Too dangerous, particularly since you refuse to see a doctor."

He struggled upright onto his elbows. "Then we might as well put this time to good use. Bring me up to speed on the major cases we worked together."

"Are you sure you're up to listening?"

"Concentrating will keep me awake, and maybe we can figure out who's after us."

"Where should I start?"

"What was the last case we worked together?"

"The Maitland kidnapping."

Gritting his teeth against the ache in his arm and the pounding in his head and struggling to stay awake, Stephen listened as Rachel filled in the details of the rescue of Margaret Maitland and the subsequent deaths of her kidnappers. Although he had been a major participant in the events, as he heard them described, they seemed as if they'd happened to someone else.

That Stephen Chandler was a total stranger.

"Margaret Maitland's fine now," Rachel concluded. "I saw her picture in the *Charlotte Observer* a few weeks ago, taken when she and her husband attended a charity event there. They're expecting their first child soon.''

''With the kidnappers dead and Margaret safe, doesn't look like there's anyone left to hold a grudge against us.''

Rachel shrugged. ''Margaret's father never trusted her husband. Claimed he married her for her wealth. If her husband set up the kidnapping to get Margaret's money, he could be furious that we foiled his plans to claim the ransom *and* his wife's inheritance.''

''If Maitland's driving motivation is greed, I can't see him paying a hit man's going rate, just for revenge on us. Too expensive.''

''You could be right,'' she said. ''And it's too risky for him to attempt revenge himself. He has a pretty cushy setup in Savannah. He could ruin everything if he were caught.''

''What's the next case?'' An unidentifiable sound in a room off the living area caught his attention and he stiffened in alarm. ''Did you hear that?''

''It's okay.'' Rachel smiled and shoved to her feet. ''It's my daughter. If she's awake, she's probably hungry.''

''Your daughter? You're married?'' Somehow that possibility hadn't entered his short-circuited mind. Why was the thought so disappointing?

Rachel's smile clouded. ''I'm not married. It didn't work out.''

''I shouldn't have asked. It's none of my business.''

She started to disagree, then stopped. ''Don't go to sleep. I'll be right back.''

Knowing he was close to dropping off, he propped himself on his elbows to await her return.

You've really screwed things up big-time. No memory. A gunshot wound. And a woman and child depending on you to keep them safe, when you can't remember your own name, much less who's out to kill you.

Frustrated and exhausted, he dropped back onto the pillows. In seconds he was sound asleep.

RACHEL PUSHED OPEN the bright plaid curtains, and the delicate, rosy light of dawn flooded the small bedroom. She and Stephen had talked the night away. Her daughter lay awake behind the barricade of pillows, kicking her chubby legs and grinning in the sunny manner that always melted Rachel's heart.

"Good morning, pumpkin. Are you hungry?"

Jessica shook her head from side to side, her newest response in answer to everything.

Rachel leaned over and tickled her tummy. "You don't fool me. You love to eat as much as your father—" She clamped her lips shut. She'd have to be careful what she said with Stephen in the next room.

Jessica giggled beneath her touch, stretched and gazed up with adoration in her deep brown eyes. Stephen's eyes. At least, thanks to his amnesia, Rachel didn't have to explain about Jessica or worry that he'd guess the child was his. Relieving her of that torment was the only good thing about his loss of memory.

With efficiency born of practice, she stripped off Jessica's clothes and bathed her with a warm, damp cloth before dressing her in the last set of clean clothes from the diaper bag. She scooped her daughter into her arms and carried her into the living room, steeling herself for Stephen's first sight of his daughter.

On the sofa, Stephen lay unmoving, eyes closed, the well-developed muscles of his chest rising and falling in the gentle rhythm of sleep.

With a strangled shout, she rushed to him. "Stephen, wake up!"

Her cry startled Jessica, who began to wail.

To Rachel's relief, he opened his eyes and blinked in confusion. "What's going on?"

"This is Jessica. She's hungry."

When his bleary gaze focused on the child in her arms, his expression transformed, softened, and his dark eyes brightened. "Hello, kiddo."

At the sound of his voice, Jessica ceased sobbing, cast him a dazzling smile and held out her arms.

His reciprocal grin reflected his pleasure. "She likes me. May I hold her?"

"Your arm—"

"I have one good one. I can manage. I love kids."

Rachel's throat clogged with emotion as she lowered her daughter into Stephen's arm. Although they'd never discussed the subject of children, she should have guessed his affinity for them. Whenever they'd interviewed children, Stephen had always established an immediate rapport, setting them at ease with his open friendliness. The youngsters somehow perceived his innate caring and cooperated with him, even when other law enforcement officers had been unable to get a word out of them.

As far back as her days at the academy, Rachel had noted that law enforcement seemed to draw recruits from two distinct personality types, those who yearned for the power and authority of the badge and the opportunity for dominance it often provided, and those who truly cared about people and wanted to help them. Stephen epitomized the latter category.

"How you doing, sweetheart?" he crooned to Jessica.

Jessica snuggled happily into the crook of his arm, reached up, and patted the dark stubble on his cheek with pudgy fingers. His expression as he contemplated his daughter made Rachel's knees weak.

"She likes me," he repeated without taking his eyes off the little girl.

"Children at that age are indiscriminate in their affection," she replied, more sharply than she'd intended, and instantly regretted her loss of control.

He raised his head and narrowed his eyes, assessing her with a questioning glance.

"Sorry." She could feel the heat creeping up her neck and face. "I didn't mean to snap. I'm a bear when I don't get my sleep."

"No problem. I'll hold her while you fix her breakfast."

Rachel returned to the bedroom, dug into Jessica's carryall for formula and a bottle and returned to the living room. She halted in the doorway, mesmerized by the sight of Stephen with Jessica in his arms. He was obviously enchanted by his daughter. Judging from Jessica's giggles of delight, the feeling was mutual.

Rachel considered telling him the truth, but discarded the thought as quickly as it came. Stephen was engaged, perhaps even married by now. For all she knew, Anne Michelle could be expecting a child of their own. Rachel had to stay the course she'd taken over a year ago. Once she and Stephen had dealt with the threat that stalked them, she and Jessica would go their own way and not see him again. It was better like that. For everybody.

She stepped into the living room and approached the sofa.

Stephen nodded at the bottle in her hand. "May I feed her?"

Unable to think of a reason to refuse, Rachel handed him the bottle. "I'll fix your breakfast. You need to rebuild your strength."

She tore her gaze from the sight of Jessica nestled in the crook of his right arm, her tiny hands clasping his big one that held her bottle, and hurried into the kitchen before he could spot the tears in her eyes.

Thrusting sentimental notions away, she browsed the cabinets and freezer, searching for breakfast ingredients. Whoever owned the cabin kept it well stocked. Within minutes she had oatmeal with cinnamon and raisins simmering on the stove and sausage patties sizzling in a frying pan.

She placed dishes and flatware on the table beside a window that overlooked the valley and distant mountain ridges. It was going to be one of those perfect autumn days, cool and crisp, without a cloud in the sky.

Perfect, except for the faceless danger that stalked them.

Later, after she had put Jessica down for her morning nap and washed the breakfast dishes, she joined Stephen, who sat in a comfortable chair before the fire, eyes closed, his skin pale in spite of his tan. He opened his eyes at her approach and smiled with a warmth that hit her like a mule kick, bringing home with a vengeance how much she'd missed him.

"Tell me about our other cases," he said.

"Are you sure you're up to this? You should be resting." She sank into the chair opposite him.

"I can rest later. For now, we should compile a list of likely suspects."

"We worked another kidnapping, right before Margaret Maitland's, a two-day-old infant stolen from County Hospital while her mother was sleeping." Her stomach knotted at the memory. Only now that she had Jessica could she truly understand the panic and devastation of the parents at the disappearance of their child.

"Did we find her?"

"Hospital security cameras captured on video an unknown couple, a young woman and middle-aged man, wandering the halls of the maternity wing. We gave the tape to local television stations, and they ran it on the evening news. Within minutes we had a call from the owner of a motel on I-95. He recognized the couple."

"They'd registered under their real names?"

She shook her head. "Too smart for that, but not smart enough. We picked up prints off the motel registration card. They belonged to Willard Straith of Clover, South Carolina.''

"He had a record?"

"His prints were on file because he worked in a defense plant outside Rock Hill. With agents from the Charlotte and Columbia offices, we surrounded his house. Our primary goal was to retrieve the baby—unharmed.''

That day was etched in her mind forever. Stephen had been first through the door. While others subdued the couple, he had gathered the infant in his arms and carried her outside to safety. A photographer had caught him emerging from the house, the tiny baby appearing even more minuscule in the muscular arms of the six-foot-two agent. But it was the tenderness on Stephen's face that had captured the attention of newspaper editors around the country and won the hearts of women all over the nation. For weeks afterward, he'd received hundreds of love letters and proposals of marriage.

"Did we?" he broke into her reminiscence.

"Did we what?"

"Find the baby safe?"

She told him about the rescue and his resulting notoriety.

"What happened to the kidnappers?" he asked.

"They were convicted and sentenced three months ago. The news was carried in the local papers.''

He looked thoughtful. "Could they have hired someone to carry out their revenge?"

"I doubt it. First of all, they were dirt poor. And they weren't vindictive people. It was sad, really.

They wanted a baby so bad, they weren't thinking straight.''

"What about the women who wrote to me? Could one of them be our threat? 'Hell hath no fury' and all that?''

She grinned. ''You handled that situation well. You hired a secretarial firm to send a letter to everyone who wrote to you—a very pleasant form letter—and you signed each one personally. There were probably a lot of disappointed females as a result, but I can't imagine one enraged enough to turn murderous.''

"Stranger things have been known to happen.''

Rachel shook her head. ''If this threat came from one of your admirers, why would she come after me?''

"Jealousy?'' His dark eyes twinkled. ''After all, you were my partner.''

"But anyone who knew us would have told her we were just friends,'' she insisted quickly. Her heart ached with how much she'd missed him these past long months.

"Anyone who obsesses over a newspaper photo of a stranger is a few sandwiches short of a picnic. We're not talking logic here. Did I keep a list of the names and addresses?''

She laughed. ''Absolutely. You're a world-class pack rat. You never throw anything away. Not even when you had to pay to have it hauled to Atlanta when you moved.''

He didn't return her smile. ''If the list is at my place in Atlanta, it doesn't do us much good here.''

"I know." She sighed. "Maybe I should contact Jason or Stan."

"Who are they?"

"Jason Bender and Stan Lewolsky—agents we worked with in the Savannah office. We could ask them to help us."

"No!" His shout reverberated off the cabin walls. He glanced guiltily toward the room where Jessica slept, then said in a lower tone, "Don't ask how I know, but something tells me not to trust anybody."

"Trust no one?" She didn't know whether to laugh or cry. "No wonder they call you Mulder behind your back."

"Mulder? *The X-Files* guy?" He slammed his fist against the arm of the chair. "How the hell can I remember TV trivia, but not the things that are important?"

"The brain's a mysterious thing. Even now, medical science is only beginning to map its functions." She leaned toward him and covered his fist with her hand. "Let me take you to a doctor."

"My instincts nix that idea, too."

Reluctantly she drew her hand from his comforting warmth. "Your instincts were always on target. We'll have to go with them. For now, they're all we've got."

They sat in silence, the only sound in the room the occasional pop and hiss of the fire. Stephen stared at the flames as if searching for answers there. Under different circumstances, the two of them in a cozy mountain cabin on a glorious fall day could have been relaxing and fun, but the knowledge that a killer was on their trail stole all the pleasure from the day.

"Were we ever threatened by any of the criminals we put away?" Stephen finally asked.

Rachel searched her memory. "A couple of them made death threats. Kevin Larson swore he'd kill us both."

"Where is he now?"

"The federal penitentiary." She smiled, remembering. "Even if he wasn't, he wouldn't be much of a threat. He was too big a klutz."

"What was his crime?"

"He robbed a branch bank on the outskirts of Savannah, but we were waiting for him when he reached his home."

"We were that good?" Stephen lifted his dark brows in amazement.

She shook her head. "Larson was that stupid. He was in such a hurry to escape, he dropped his wallet in the bank parking lot. We showed the photo on his driver's license to the tellers, who identified him. Then we drove to the address on his license. We arrived an hour ahead of him. He'd stopped at a supermarket to buy cleansers to remove the ink from the bank's dye pack from his clothes and car."

Stephen ran his fingers through his thick hair and winced when they grazed the knot on his temple. His frustration was evident. "Anyone else make threats?"

"Johnny Slade, but he's in the federal pen, too."

"On what charges?"

"Racketeering and money laundering. This guy's vicious, and he has connections with the mob."

"A mob hit man might have used the .22 caliber that shot me."

"It's possible, but if true, it means we really are dealing with a nameless, faceless killer."

Stephen's features contorted suddenly with pain.

"What is it?" she asked. "Your head?"

"My arm. Hurts like the devil."

"I'll get you more painkillers. And it's time I changed that bandage."

Retrieving the first aid kit from the kitchen, she shuddered at the possibility of a mob hit man on their trail. A hired assassin was devoid of compassion, a man who could kill a child with as little remorse as he felt for his adult victims. She had to get Jessica away from here, to safety. She checked on her daughter, whose sleep was undisturbed by the danger that stalked them, and returned to Stephen.

"Take off your shirt," she said.

With his right hand, he unfastened the buttons of the plaid flannel shirt, then shrugged it off his shoulders. She couldn't help wondering what all those lovestruck women would have thought if they'd seen *this* picture on the front page of their newspaper. She tore her gaze from the delicious sight of his bare chest and focused on his wounded arm. The bandage was barely soiled, a sign that the bleeding had ceased.

While he sat stoically beneath her care, she cut the gauze away, cleaned his wound and applied a fresh bandage. She handed him more caplets and a glass of water.

"We have to talk," she said after he'd swallowed them.

"I thought that's what we've been doing."

"Not about cases." She settled again into the chair across from him. "About Jessica."

He cocked his head to one side in a gesture that swamped her with memories. "Jessica?"

"She isn't safe here."

"We don't know that for sure."

"If a mob hit man is after me and she's *with* me, she isn't safe."

He leaned back against the headrest. "What do you suggest?"

"I want to take her to my parents in Raleigh."

"Not a good idea."

"It's the best I can think of." She set her mouth in a determined line.

"Is it?" His dark eyes bored into hers. "What if someone's staking out your parents' place, hoping you'll show up? You could put yourself, your parents and Jessica in danger by going there."

"So I just sit here and wait? This cabin is safe only as long as no one knows we're here, and with your memory gone, we can't be sure of that. And, if someone does come after us, there's only one road off the mountain. We'd be cut off, without escape."

"We're both armed." He nodded toward the shoulder holster with his Glock pistol she had hung across a ladder-back chair.

"My point, exactly. I don't want Jessica caught in a cross fire." She yawned, fighting the cumulative effects of twenty-four hours without sleep. "Without your memory, you can't tell me whether anyone knows we're here. I don't want Jessica at risk."

"Taking her to Raleigh places her at risk, and you, too." He leaned toward her and placed his hand on her knee. "You're exhausted. You'll think more clearly after you've had some sleep."

"If I sleep, what will keep you from dozing off again?"

His expression turned grim. "Knowing someone's out there, looking for us."

She would have argued with him, but she was too tired. "Wake me in a couple hours, okay?"

He nodded, and she went into the bedroom, curled up beside her slumbering daughter and almost instantly dropped off to sleep.

She dreamed of hordes of men in camouflage clothes and balaclavas, storming the mountaintop. She and Stephen fought them off until their ammunition ran out.

"Take Jessica and run!" Stephen shouted.

"Where is she? I can't find her."

Awaking with a start, she reached for her daughter, but the bed was empty. The acrid taste of fear filled her mouth, and her pulse raced in panic. She had been asleep for hours, judging from the angle of the sunlight in the room. How long had Jessica been gone?

She leaped to her feet and dashed into the living room. It, too, was deserted.

Jessica and Stephen were gone.

Chapter Five

Where had they gone?

Her heart pounded as her mind raced, envisioning all kinds of scenarios—all of them too frightening to contemplate. Had Stephen taken Jessica, or had someone else abducted them both?

Fearing the worst, Rachel raced across the living room to the front door. Her car and Stephen's were still parked in the drive.

"Come out and join us," a voice called to her.

With her heart thudding in her ears, she stepped onto the broad front porch. In the northwest corner, where sunlight puddled on the weathered floorboards, Jessica sat in a playpen, cooing to Poochie, her favorite stuffed animal. Stephen reclined in an Adirondack chair only inches away.

"It's a gorgeous day," he called to her. "Come out with us." Embarrassed by her momentary panic, Rachel crossed to the porch rail and gazed at the panoramic view. Spread below her, the valley stretched in a gaudy patchwork of autumn russets, yellows and greens. Along the skyline, the peaks of the Smoky

Mountains jutted sharply against the cloudless sky, free of the customary haze that had given them their name.

She allowed the breeze to cool her heated face for a few minutes before she curled into the chair beside Stephen's.

"How's your head?" she asked.

"Better, thanks."

"And your memory?"

He grimaced. "Still a blank slate."

Part of her hoped he wouldn't remember anything until she and Jessica were back home, safe not only from the person who stalked them but from Stephen's shrewd observations. "Where did you find the play-pen?"

"In the laundry room off the kitchen. The owner must have children."

"Do you remember? After all, meeting here was your idea."

He shook his head. "But we can easily find out."

"How?"

"While you were sleeping, I called the telephone company, gave them the number of the phone in the cabin, and they provided the name the phone's listed under. George Windham. Ring any bells?"

She shook her head. "Never heard of him."

"I also called the Jackson County Courthouse—"

"You were supposed to be resting."

He grinned. "I was supposed to stay awake, remember? The only way to keep from dozing off was to keep busy."

"How did you manage to lift Jessica without waking me?"

His smile widened. "As hard as you were sleeping, an eight-hundred-pound gorilla wouldn't have disturbed you. When I heard the baby gurgling and cooing to herself, I brought her out here so you could rest longer."

Rachel's cheeks blazed again at the idea of Stephen watching her sleep. Anxious to change the subject, she said, "Anyway, I'm sorry I don't recognize the name George Windham."

"I was hoping he was someone from the Bureau, someone we could trust."

"He could be an agent assigned to the Atlanta office and I've just never met him."

Stephen frowned. "I'm guessing he's retired. His legal residence is Bonita Springs, Florida."

"Bonita Springs?"

"You know the place?"

"That's where your mother lived, until her death three years ago."

"So Windham could be a friend of my mother's?"

"Maybe you should call him and find out."

He wrinkled his brow, considering. "We shouldn't reveal our hiding place until we know who's after us."

"That's the paradox. How can we learn who's after us *without* disclosing our location?"

He reached across the gap between their chairs and grasped her hand. "Rachel?"

Her name sounded foreign on his lips. For years he'd seldom called her anything but Doc. She recalled the days, weeks, years she had spent with him, taking their friendship for granted.

Dear God, she'd missed him.

Achingly aware of his strong fingers twined with hers, she gazed into the golden-brown mirror of his eyes. "Yes?"

"Tell me about myself."

"What do you want to know?"

"Do I have family? Someone who's worried about me, wondering where I am?"

"I'm...not sure."

"What's that supposed to mean?"

She tugged her hand from the mesmerizing warmth of his grip. "I told you, we...lost touch over a year ago. I heard rumors—"

"What kind of rumors?"

"That you'd met someone and were engaged to be married. Does the name Anne Michelle Logan mean anything to you?"

He thought for a moment, then shook his head.

"Did I?" he asked.

"Marry?" She forced her gaze away from him and stared at the distant mountaintops. "I don't know. Certainly enough time has passed since I heard the rumors."

He glanced at his left hand. "I'm not wearing a ring."

"Some men don't. And in some aspects of an agent's job, a ring can be a hazard."

Out of the corner of her eye, she caught his puzzled frown. "So it's possible I have a wife in Atlanta who's waiting for me, wondering why I haven't come home or checked in?''

She nodded. ''But she's probably not worried yet. FBI spouses are used to their mates disappearing without contact for days at a time. It goes with the job.''

He shook his head. ''I don't think so.''

''It's true. That's why a lot of guys drop out. Their families can't take the uncertainty.''

''That's not what I meant. I was talking about having a wife. It doesn't feel right.''

She shrugged in an attempt to appear nonchalant and hide the surge of happiness his words shot through her before common sense jerked her back to reality. Of course it didn't feel right to him. How could he perceive love for a woman he couldn't remember? ''Do you want me to call her? Let her know you're okay?''

''Too dangerous. If someone's looking for me, he's probably watching my house.'' He bolted upright in his chair. ''If I have a wife, that means she's in danger, too.''

''Whoa, buster.'' Rachel rose and pressed his shoulders against the back of the chair. ''Take it easy. You don't want that arm to start bleeding again.''

''But my wife—''

His words pierced her heart with sadness, and she silently berated herself for her foolishness. Stephen was her friend, for Pete's sake. Jealousy had no place in their relationship. ''Knowing you as I do, I can guarantee you wouldn't have left your wife in danger.

You would have made arrangements for her safety before you left Atlanta.''

His breathing slowed, and he relaxed beneath her grip. She released him and settled into her chair once again.

''What else do you know about me, Doc?''

''Doc?'' Her pulse accelerated at the familiar nickname. ''You remember?''

His forehead crinkled in confusion. ''I was referring to the way you take care of me. What should I remember?''

She blushed. ''You seldom called me Rachel. I was always Doc to you.''

''Why 'Doc'?''

''I joined the Bureau after med school.''

''No wonder you know your way around a gunshot wound. Any idea what my chances are of getting my memory back?''

She shook her head. ''That depends on what's causing your amnesia, and I can't determine the source without X rays and other tests.''

''Then you'll have to provide my memories for me.''

''What do you want to know?''

''Who am I?''

''I've told you. If you don't believe me, there's plenty of identification in your wallet.''

''Guess I phrased that wrong. I know my name. I want to know more.''

''You're thirty-four, born in Philadelphia, undergraduate and law degrees from Harvard, went directly from law school to the FBI Academy at Quantico.

Your first assignment was Tampa, then Baton Rouge, Nashville and Savannah. You transferred sixteen months ago to Atlanta.''

"Family?"

"You were an only child. Both your parents died several years ago."

He twined his fingers through hers again. "Vital statistics don't tell me much about my character."

"What do you want to know?"

"Any skeletons in my closet?"

"You haven't broken any laws, if that's what you're worried about." She grinned. "You're so squeaky clean, you could be the poster boy for Truth, Justice and the American Way."

"Then why is somebody after me?" He slammed his other hand on the arm of the chair, and Jessica jumped in the playpen beside him.

"Sorry, sweetheart." He leaned over and tousled her dark curls before turning back to Rachel.

Not wanting to grow accustomed to the comfort of his touch, Rachel untangled her fingers from his. "If you've antagonized anyone, it's from doing your job *too* well."

To avoid his piercing glance, she looked out across the front lawn and caught sight of his government-issue sedan. She remembered how frightened she felt last night when it came up the road, and how worried she became when she saw Stephen shot, bleeding and in pain.

"Oh, my God!" she shouted and jumped to her feet. "I forgot your car!"

"What?"

"In the midst of everything last night, I didn't search your car. Maybe there's something inside that'll tell us who's after us."

Stephen started to rise from his chair, but she pushed him back with a firm hand on his shoulder. "You rest and keep an eye on Jessica. I'll search."

She bounded down the porch steps and flagstone walk to the vehicle. In her haste to get him inside last night, she'd left the keys in the ignition. She removed them and checked the trunk first. Aside from the usual tools and emergency equipment, the trunk held only a traveling kit and garment bag with a clean suit and change of shirt that most agents kept on hand for overnight assignments. She also found a laptop computer. A thorough search of the kit and garment bag revealed nothing helpful.

A check of the back seat also proved futile. Unfortunately, Stephen's pack rat habits hadn't extended to his vehicle. She circled the car to the front passenger seat and opened the glove box. After sifting through a cluttered jumble of maps and receipts, most weeks old, she was ready to admit defeat.

His cell phone lay on the floor mat. She retrieved it and slipped it into the pocket of her jeans, grabbed the kit and garment bag from the trunk and slung the strap of the laptop's carrying case over her shoulder.

"Looks like you found something," Stephen called from the porch. "Need a hand?"

"You have a wounded arm, remember? Besides, I've wrestled grocery bags heavier than this load."

She carried his clothes and kit into the main bedroom, set the laptop and phone on the dining table and returned to the porch. Jessica sat with her face pressed against the woven side of the playpen, fascinated by butterflies flitting among the bright purple dahlias that bordered the porch. Stephen was watching her as if he hadn't a care in the world. Rachel wondered if he'd lost his worries with his memory.

She propped her hips against the porch rail and folded her arms across her chest. The burden of their safety pressed on her with the weight of the mountain beneath her, and she was desperate to identify who was after them.

"Find anything significant?" he asked.

"Not unless there's information in your laptop."

"Should we take a look?"

She was too tired, too edgy, too worried about Jessica to concentrate. "We can try but I'm having trouble thinking straight, with Jessica in danger. I want to send her to Dr. and Mrs. Kidbrough. They're my godparents, and they live near Mom and Dad. No one will be watching them or tapping their phone. I'll ask them to meet us somewhere between here and Raleigh, and they can take Jessica home with them."

Her spirits fell when she gazed at her daughter, playing happily in the sunshine. As much as Rachel wanted her safe, being separated from her baby would be the hardest thing she had ever done.

"Rachel?"

She lifted her gaze to find his dark eyes studying her. "Yes?"

"Will Jessica go with them, without being upset?"

"She was around the Kidbroughs a lot whenever

we spent time at my parents' place. She should be all right.''

"Will *you* be okay?''

He'd seen her distress over the upcoming separation as clearly as if she'd stamped it in tall letters across her forehead. ''I don't want to leave her, but what choice do I have? I can't risk her life by keeping her with me.''

He nodded, his handsome face a picture of compassion. ''Then the sooner, the better. Call the Kidbroughs and set up a meeting.''

''You shouldn't be traveling, and I can't leave you here, not without memories to warn who's a threat and who isn't.''

''If you drive, I can travel all right. Getting away from here may jog my memory.''

''But—''

''Call the Kidbroughs.''

She remembered that look of his, the obstinate set of his square jaw, the determined glint in his eyes. She might as well argue with a fence post. Without further discussion she went inside and dialed the Kidbroughs' number.

From his chair on the porch, Stephen could hear her voice, low and urgent, but he couldn't make out what she way saying. Her words had a soothing quality that lifted his spirits, like listening to a favorite song. A sudden discomfort pricked his conscience. If Rachel was right, and he had a wife back in Atlanta, why did he feel so moved by everything about the woman inside the cabin?

He glanced at Jessica, who had fallen asleep in the

playpen. Pondering his situation did little good without memories to serve him. He had to *do* something to protect this little girl and her mother.

After tugging the playpen into the shade, he sauntered off the porch to his car. Rachel had cleaned out the vehicle, except for the glove box. He withdrew the maps stashed there, selected one of the Southeast and spread it over the hood. She had mentioned the cabin was outside of Glenville, North Carolina. After a few minutes scrutiny of the small print, he located the tiny community near the South Carolina line, tucked in a valley between two mountain ranges with only one major roadway leading in and out.

If their pursuers caught up with them, they'd be trapped like rats in a box unless Stephen could find another way out of the valley. He studied the map, memorizing names and places of secondary roads that led over the mountains and connected with other highways. Even if some of those roads were unpaved, Rachel's Explorer had four-wheel drive and should get them through safely.

What worried him most, however, was the single road off this mountain. Other routes out of the valley were worthless if he and Rachel couldn't get off the mountaintop. Struggling to stay awake and ignoring the pain in his arm, Stephen tramped around the cabin, searching for any other avenues of escape.

His efforts were rewarded when he spotted the ruts of an old logging road, leading off the far side of the mountain behind the cabin. The ruts, overgrown with weeds and filled with dead leaves, disappeared over a ridge, and he couldn't be certain the road didn't dead-end somewhere on the mountainside. If nothing else, however, the logging road might present a place to hide in an emergency.

Satisfied that he'd learned the lay of the land around the cabin, he tramped back to the front. The savory aroma of soup greeted him as he climbed onto the porch.

"Lunch is ready," Rachel called through the open door.

Jessica was still sleeping, so he pulled her playpen inside. Rachel was placing bowls of steaming vegetable soup and a basket of hot corn muffins on the table. With her cheeks flushed from the heat of the stove and a lock of blond hair falling over one eye, she was an appealing picture of domesticity.

Except for the holstered gun slung under her shoulder.

"Did you reach the Kidbroughs?" He went to the kitchen sink to wash his hands.

Rachel slid into a seat at the table and began buttering a muffin. "They'll meet us at five o'clock this afternoon at the entrance to the Biltmore Estate near Asheville. They plan to spend the night in Asheville, then drive back to Raleigh with Jessica tomorrow."

He dried his hands and joined her. "Did you tell them to warn your parents that they and their house might be under surveillance?"

"I explained as much as I could—as much as I know." Suddenly, she shoved back her chair, hurried across the room and returned with a photograph. "I almost forgot. While I was on the phone, I found this in the desk drawer when I was searching for a pencil.''

She handed him the snapshot. Its colors were faded, and from the style of the subjects' clothing and hair, he guessed the picture was at least twenty years old. An attractive woman in her forties with dark hair and eyes stood beside an older, heavyset man with graying hair in front of the cabin. The family resemblance between the pair was obvious.

He turned the photo over. On the back was scrawled, ''Dear Uncle George, here's a print of the picture I took of you and Mom with my new camera. Love, Stephen.''

He raised his head and threw Rachel a questioning glance.

''That's your mother,'' she said. ''I met her when she visited you in Savannah. George must be her brother. They certainly look enough alike.''

The connection clicked in place. ''Uncle George is George Windham. This place belongs to my uncle.''

''Makes sense. That's why you thought we'd be safe here. Because the cabin's in your uncle's name, it isn't connected to you in any way. You could easily draw me a map from memory, and you knew it would be well stocked and that the extra key would be under the third rock from the porch steps.''

''You made the connection quickly,'' he said, and an uneasy thought struck him. ''Wonder who else knows I have an uncle George?''

''I worked with you four years and never knew.''

''But you never had any reason to trace my family tree.''

She wiped her fingers on her napkin and considered him with frightened eyes. "You think the people who're after us will check out your relatives?"

He didn't want to scare her, but they had to face facts. "If they're desperate enough, they'll do whatever it takes to find us." He slammed his fist against his palm in frustration. Why had he chosen this place? Was it really safe to stay? If only he could remember.

"What if you called your uncle before you called me and asked if you could use his cabin?"

"What do you mean?"

"If you did, maybe you told him who's after us. Why don't you call him? Maybe he can help."

He shook his head. "What could I say? He would recognize my voice, but with my memory gone, he couldn't be sure it's me on the other end of the line."

"Okay." She sipped a spoonful of soup. "I'll call him."

"And say what?" he asked with an ironic laugh. "That you're staying in his mountain house with his nephew, who won't talk to him because he can't remember anything? He'll think you're crazy."

She set down her spoon and glared. "I will definitely go crazy if we don't find out who's after us. It's like living in a bad dream."

She was magnificent when she was angry. Her eyes sparked with green fire, the color rose again in her cheeks, and her shapely chest heaved with indignation. Could he have worked with such a woman for four years and not noticed? He glanced at Jessica in her playpen. Or maybe he had noticed, but Jessica's daddy had beat him to the prize.

He held up his hands in surrender. "All right, have it your way. Call Uncle George and see what he can tell us."

She rose to her feet and hurried to the phone. After a call to information for George Windham's number in Florida, she dialed his home.

"Mr. Windham?" she asked. "I'm Rachel Goforth, a friend of your nephew Stephen Chandler. I've been trying to locate him, but the Bureau office in Atlanta either doesn't know where he is or won't tell me."

She paused, listening to Windham's long response. Her eyes widened and her eyebrows lifted in surprise. "You're certain?"

"Certain of what?" Stephen asked, but she shook her head at him without answering.

"Thanks for your help, Mr. Windham.... Yes, if I find Stephen, I'll have him call you."

She replaced the receiver and stared at him in disbelief. "He says he hasn't talked with you in several weeks."

"That's it? He took a hell of a long time saying it."

"There's more." She settled in the chair across from him. "Someone from the Atlanta office called him this morning, asking how to find you."

"That sounds reasonable, since I didn't show up for work today, and George Windham is probably listed as my next of kin."

She raised her eyebrows again. "Not if you're married. You forgot your Anne Michelle."

"Among several hundred other things. But I see your point. What did Uncle George tell this person?"

"The caller asked if he knew where you might go to get away from it all. George told him about this cabin. We're not safe here anymore."

"Don't jump to conclusions—"

"I'm not." She pushed to her feet and went back to the phone. After another call to long-distance and a request for the Atlanta office of the FBI, she dialed again.

"May I speak with Agent Ken Danford?" As she listened to the response, her eyebrows drew together in a frown. "You're sure? Sorry, guess someone gave me bad information."

"What was that all about?" Stephen demanded when she'd hung up.

The color had disappeared from her cheeks, and her hands were shaking. "Your uncle George said the agent who called said he was Ken Danford. The receptionist at the Atlanta office insists there's no one there by that name. If it wasn't an agent from your office trying to locate you—"

"Then whoever's after us knows where we are. Get your things together. We're leaving now."

He rushed into the main bedroom where Rachel had placed his belongings. A quick check of the closet revealed men's jeans, shirts and boots that looked as if they'd fit. He filled his arms with clothes, grabbed the garment bag and kit and hurried to the Explorer.

Passing Rachel with her arms loaded with Jessica's things, he ran back to the house for his computer, cell phone and the maps he'd brought in from his car. On a rack beside the door hung a man's heavy jacket. He snatched the garment and shrugged it on over his holstered gun.

Rachel joined him with Jessica in her arms. "Ready?"

"Can you drive? My arm—"

"No problem, but let's move."

Together they raced to the Explorer. While Rachel strapped Jessica in the child carrier in the back seat, Stephen scanned the mountainside and the valley below.

Sunlight glinted off a windshield as a vehicle left the highway and started up the road to the cabin.

"They've found us," he said.

Chapter Six

"Looks like we'll have to do this the hard way," Stephen said.

"We can't shoot our way out." Rachel cast a panicked look at her daughter, who gazed at her mother from the carrier with innocent, trusting eyes. "That only works in the movies. If this encounter deteriorates into a battle, I'll surrender and beg for Jessica's life."

"It won't come to that," Stephen said with infuriating calm. "Get in the car."

"But—"

"No arguments. Get in."

Stephen hopped into the passenger side. Unable to think of a better alternative, Rachel climbed into the driver's seat and started the engine.

He jerked his head toward the gravel road that snaked down the mountain several miles in a series of sharp switchbacks. "How long will it take them to cover the distance from the valley?"

"Ten minutes, maybe less."

"Pull the car behind the cabin."

"Are you crazy? We can't hide a vehicle this size—"

"Drive!"

Shaking her head at his obstinacy, she put the SUV in gear, backed out of the parking area and drove up the sloping bank of the cabin's side yard. The Explorer's four-wheel drive made the climb easily, and as she maneuvered around the corner into the backyard, Stephen pointed to an almost imperceptible break in the trees.

"There's a road."

"Where?"

"Not much of one, but if you look close between those two large hickories, you'll see it. Follow it as far as you can." He threw open his door and jumped to the ground.

"Where are you going?"

"To cover our tracks. I'll catch up with you down the mountain. Now *go!*"

In the back seat, Jessica began to cry. Rachel didn't need further encouragement to take her daughter as far from the approaching danger as fast as possible, but even as she did as he ordered, plunging the vehicle into the underbrush along the rutted road, she hated leaving Stephen behind. In most circumstances he could take care of himself, but with his wounded arm and loss of memory, he was no match for a trained killer. But she had no choice. She had to get Jessica to safety.

With a sob of desperation, she increased her speed as much as the uncertain terrain allowed. Glad for the vehicle's hunter-green finish that blended with the evergreens, she eased the SUV between the trees along the overgrown path that looked more like a rain-washed gully than a road. The vehicle bucked and pitched on the uneven surface. Jessica ceased sobbing and giggled with delight at the bumpy ride.

Low-hanging branches whipped across the wind-shield, momentarily obscuring Rachel's view. In the rearview mirror, she could see Stephen, sweeping tire tracks from the red clay dust of the cabin yard with an evergreen branch and filling the ruts in the logging road with dead leaves. Then the road dipped over a ridge and she lost sight of him.

Rachel kept driving, but the farther down the mountain she progressed, the more obstructed the road became. Oblivious of the damage to her car, she crashed through head-high thickets of blackberry brambles and thick undergrowth. At one point she had to climb out and drag a rotted tree trunk from the road. At another, she crushed a maroon-leafed dog-wood seedling in her path.

She halted and looked behind her. No sign of Stephen. Or anyone else. A glance at her watch indicated only seven minutes had passed since she'd left the cabin. It seemed like an eternity.

She continued down the mountain, flinching at every whine of the motor, every pop of a broken branch. Sound traveled for miles in the mountains and could proclaim their presence as clearly as a neon sign.

Halfway down the slope, she maneuvered around another sharp switchback and discovered, hollowed into the red clay of the mountainside, an opening large enough for a vehicle to pull into while another passed on the one-lane road. She backed the Explorer into the makeshift cavern, killed the engine and rolled down her window a few inches.

She would wait for Stephen here. Exhausted and weak as he was from loss of blood and lack of sleep, she doubted he'd have the stamina to continue much farther down the mountain on foot.

If he made it this far.

Drawing the automatic from beneath her jacket, she operated the slide, chambered a bullet and waited. Thankful that her FBI training kept her focused so that fears didn't overwhelm her, she listened for Stephen's approach. He should be joining her soon.

She turned up the collar of her jacket against the cold seeping in the window. A keening wind tossed the tree branches, rustled piles of dead leaves, and lifted them in swirling eddies. From a distance came the splashing of a creek as it cascaded down the mountainside toward the lake below. From even farther away, the whine of a chain saw carried on the breeze.

In the midst of all those noises, someone could approach the car and she would never hear his movements, even with the window open. At least the cavern protected her on three sides, and she could spot anyone approaching from the front.

Where was Stephen?

She looked at her watch again. Another ten minutes had passed since the last time she checked. He should have joined her by now.

Unless he isn't coming.

She discarded the possibility he might be hurt as quickly as it entered her mind, then smacked the steering wheel with her fist. He may have lost his memory, but she was certain he hadn't changed his modus operandi. Accustomed to taking risks, he'd stayed on the mountaintop to catch a glimpse of their pursuers.

What if their pursuers had sighted him first?

She longed to go back to help him, but she couldn't leave Jessica. If anything had happened to Stephen, and Rachel was also captured or killed, Jessica might never be found on this deserted mountainside.

Rachel stifled a sob and prayed.

The sun shifted behind the clouds, casting the woods in gloomy shadows, which brought with them a bone-deep chill. Rachel rolled up the window and crawled into the back seat. Grabbing the plaid blanket she kept in the back of the car, she tucked it around Jessica, who had fallen asleep again. Shivering, Rachel curled up next to her.

In less than three hours, the Kidbroughs would be waiting to pick up Jessica at the Biltmore Estate. If Stephen didn't come soon, Rachel would have to decide whether to risk returning to the cabin and taking its main road off the mountain or chancing whether the old logging road exited onto another road at the mountain's foot.

She snuggled against her daughter in an attempt to keep them both warm. In spite of her fears and the need to remain alert, she surrendered to the effects of too much stress and too many hours without sleep. She nodded off several times, only to snap to attention at an unusual sound, like the frantic barking of a dog and the lowing of cattle, carried on the wind from a farm in the valley.

I can't desert him. Not again. Not now.

The prospect of leaving Stephen behind stabbed her like a knife in the heart. But Stephen could take care of himself, her conscience argued, while Jessica needed her protection to stay alive.

Please, God, keep him safe.

She slept again, and her dreams of being chased by dark, sinister strangers returned. She whimpered in her sleep, and her heart almost stopped when a hand clamped over her mouth and another closed over her gun. She came instantly awake, but the intruder muffled her scream.

"It's okay," Stephen whispered in her ear. "It's me."

She couldn't see in the darkness, but she knew his voice. Her heart, pounding as if trying to beat its way out of her chest, slowed its racing when Stephen removed his hand from her lips.

Her joy at his arrival chased away her fear. "Are you okay?"

"Aside from being cold, hungry and exhausted," he said, the irony edging his words, "yeah, I feel terrific."

"Anyone follow you?"

"No, we're safe—for now."

"Tell me what happened back there."

"Let's get moving first. It's almost five."

She bolted upright. They had missed the rendezvous. "The Kidbroughs are waiting—"

"Do they have a car phone?"

"The number's in the address book in my purse."

"Call them. Set up another time and meeting place." He slid the cellular phone into her hands and switched on the vehicle's dome light.

She blinked in the sudden brightness. After fumbling in her purse for the address book, she found the number and punched it into the phone.

Dr. Kidbrough answered immediately. "Where are you? Are you all right?"

"We're okay, just delayed. It'll take us a few hours. Where can we meet you?"

"There's a Shoney's at the Hendersonville exit off the interstate, where we planned to stop for supper. We'll wait for you there."

"I don't know how long—"

"Don't worry. It's open all night. We'll wait as long as it takes."

The affection and reassurance in his voice brought tears to her eyes. She turned off the cell phone, handed it back to Stephen and climbed into the front seat behind the wheel. Stephen settled into the front passenger seat and fastened his seat belt with his good arm.

"We're supposed to meet the Kidbroughs in Hendersonville," she told him. "Is it safe to go back to the cabin road or should we continue this way?"

He pointed down the dark, overgrown trail. "We'll have to gamble that this old logging road eventually leads off the mountain."

Rachel pulled out of the hiding place and headed down the rutted slope. As treacherous as the descent had been earlier, in the darkness, the road seemed a hundred times worse.

As if reading her mind, he said, "If the road dead-ends, we'll hike out."

She bit back an angry reply. He was in no condition to hike anywhere, and she doubted she could travel very far carrying Jessica across the steep terrain.

"This SUV is rugged," she said. "If we run out of road, we'll blaze a new one."

"From the looks of the road behind us, that's what you've been doing all along."

"Did you see who's after us?" she asked.

"After I covered the tracks of your car, I hid beneath a pile of leaves near the parking area. A red pickup, with gun racks in the rear window pulled up. Just one man inside."

"What did he look like?"

"Tall, moved like a younger man...in his late twenties, early thirties. He was dressed in jeans, heavy jacket, work boots. A knit cap covered his hair, and he was wearing dark glasses, so I couldn't get a good look at his face. Sound like anyone you know?"

"Maybe he was a local farmer, being neighborly." Her voice shook as the Explorer lurched over a washed-out portion of the road.

"Would a neighborly farmer draw a .357 Magnum before kicking in the front door?"

She shuddered, picturing what could have happened to them if they hadn't called George Windham and been warned someone was coming for them.

"Why did you stay up there so long?" she asked,

trying to keep her voice from revealing how worried she had been.

Stephen considered her with a searching look, as if he'd picked up on the concern she'd tried to hide. "I couldn't leave until he did, and he took his sweet time turning the cabin inside out."

"Was there *anything* familiar about him?" she asked.

"Sorry. Without my memory, nothing's familiar, except…"

"What?"

"You."

"*I'm* familiar?" The caressing inflection of his voice brought a flush of warmth to her face and accelerated her pulse. "If you remember me, that's a good sign. Maybe your memories are returning."

"It's not a memory." His voice softened, warmed. "More like a feeling."

"That's only natural. We were good buddies." She was glad he couldn't see her blushing in the dark. Their conversation was treading dangerous ground.

"Did you get the pickup's license number?" she asked, steering him onto a less hazardous topic.

"I tried, but red mud caked the plate. I couldn't even tell what state the truck was registered in."

"So we're back to square one, with no idea who's after us or why." She sighed in frustration. "At least things aren't any worse."

As if to contradict her claim, the left front end of the Explorer dipped at a forty-five-degree angle, and the vehicle stopped abruptly, tossing Rachel forward. If her seat belt hadn't been fastened, she'd have done a header into the windshield. She pressed the accelerator, but the car wouldn't move.

"We're stuck," she announced.

Stephen unclasped his seat belt and opened the door. With the vehicle tilted to the left, he had to jump to reach the ground. He crossed in front of the headlights to inspect the left wheel.

Rachel lowered her window and studied the damage. "Should I try backing up?"

"Won't help." Stephen's face was pale in the glare of the headlights. "The road's washed out and the tire's dropped into a gully. Do you have a flashlight?"

She reached into the glove compartment, grabbed a Maglite, and tossed it to him. He disappeared momentarily as he inspected the underside of the car.

When he popped into view again, his face was grim. "The axle doesn't appear damaged, but there's no way we're getting out of here."

"And I guess we can't call a tow truck. So much for getting off this mountain."

She tried to exit her door, but when it had opened only a few inches the bottom edge dug into the dirt. She crawled over the passenger seat, leaped to the ground and surveyed the tilted front end of the Explorer. "Is there any way we could jack up the car enough to free it?"

Stephen knelt and scraped at the surface of the gully. Soil crumbled in his hand. "The ground is unstable. The jack won't hold."

He rose and wiped the dirt from his palms. In the glare of the headlights, the pallor of his face revealed the debilitating effects of his trek down the mountain.

Despite the growing chill of the October night, sweat beaded his forehead. Bits of leaves clung to his dark hair, remnants of his hiding place as he'd observed the gunman, and his dark eyes burned with a feverish intensity.

She stood on tiptoe to brush the debris from his hair and laid the inside of her wrist against his forehead to check for fever. His skin felt cool against hers. Too cool.

"You should get off your feet," she told him. "Doctor's orders."

He caught her hand and his gaze captured hers, riveting her with the power of his scrutiny. "One of us has to go for help, Doc. It should be me."

"You're in no condition—" In the back seat of the Explorer, Jessica began to cry. "Jess is hungry. While you feed her, I can hike down to the valley. I heard cattle earlier, so there must be a farm down there."

Reluctantly she tugged her hand from the warmth of his and climbed into the back seat with her daughter. She'd prepared a bottle so many times, even in the dark, the procedure was no challenge. But this time as she did so, she was overwhelmed by the need to get Jessica to safety with the Kidbroughs. Only then could she concentrate on the puzzle of the unidentified gunman.

For now, they had to get off the mountain.

Fast.

She couldn't think of any way around the problem except hiking down to the valley where a farmer might have a truck to pull them out.

Stephen crawled into the front seat to switch off

the headlights, then climbed over into the rear next to her and took Jessica. Before he'd extinguished the lights, the digital temperature gauge above the windshield had registered thirty-four degrees, and he shivered from the cold.

She lifted the blanket and wrapped it around Stephen and Jessica. "You'll have to bundle to keep warm."

"You'll be careful?" He grasped her hand, and his touch activated a flood of memories and a corresponding cascade of desire. Feelings she'd denied too long coursed through her, and she shoved them away, unable to think straight with his closeness so distracting.

"I should be the one starting down the mountain now," he argued.

She could hear the weariness in his voice. "You're already exhausted. If you stay with Jessica, I can cover ground faster and bring help sooner."

"Are you always this calm?" His tone was tinged with awe.

"Me, calm?" She laughed. If he only knew how her thoughts swirled, her pulse thundered with panic and her skin prickled with fear. "I put on a good front. My family was never very demonstrative, so I grew up learning to keep my feelings inside. The poker face came in handy as an FBI investigator."

"Guess that's why they called you Scully."

"You *do* remember!"

He shrugged. "Only about Scully, and that came out of nowhere."

"That's a good sign. Your other memories may start flooding back soon."

He tightened his grip on her hand, and the pressure reassured and unsettled her at the same time.

"Why did they call me Mulder?"

She smiled, remembering. "Because you have an uncanny ability to put together clues in a way no one else would think of and come up with answers. And you stick by your theories, no matter how off-the-wall they sound."

"Was I ever right?"

"You were *always* right."

He groaned. "That must have made me real popular."

"Everybody loved you."

"Everybody?"

"Now that you mention it, there were exceptions." Her pulse quickened, and she wondered what else he'd remembered. "Like the criminals you brought to justice."

"And the gunman at the cabin." He leaned back against the seat and sighed. "Why can't I remember who he is?"

"He could be a hired hit man you've never met."

Stephen flexed his wounded arm. "We'll meet soon enough. And on *my* terms. I have a score to settle."

She shivered at the deadly determination in his voice. In all the years she'd known him, Stephen had never made empty promises.

"In the meantime," he continued, "I'll make a deal with you."

"What kind of deal?"

"You hike to the farmhouse for help—"

"That's already a given."

"—and when we meet the Kidbroughs, you go with Jessica."

"What? You've got to be kidding."

"Makes sense," he insisted. "The Kidbroughs can find you both a hiding place, so you won't have to be separated from Jessica."

"And what about you?"

"I'll keep looking for whoever's after us."

"How? Your amnesia has you flying blind, like a pilot without instruments in a storm."

"I remembered the Scully bit. I'm counting on my other memories returning."

She shook her head. "Amnesia's a crazy thing. It could take years for all your memories to return—if they return at all."

"I refuse to place you and your child in more danger. I must have been crazy to have dragged you into this in the first place."

The caring in his voice warmed her. So many times in the past months, she'd longed for someone to share her burdens, someone she could trust, someone she loved—although, she attempted to assure herself, she loved him only as a good friend. Still, his concern comforted her and made her feel not only safe, but special. She hadn't felt special since Brad abandoned her at the church on her wedding day.

She wrenched herself from the spellbinding comfort of Stephen's concern. "I can't hide forever. I have a job, a child to support. The sooner I help you find who's after us, the sooner I can get back to my life."

He pulled her closer, and his hand cupped her face in the darkness. "Rachel—"

Suddenly the beams of headlights blinked as if out of nowhere on the road ahead and shot through the car.

Reacting instantly, Stephen shoved Rachel to the floor and placed Jessica in her arms. "Stay down. I'll handle this."

Light expanded inside the Explorer as the vehicle approached, and the chugging roar of an engine shattered the stillness of the night. Stephen exited the car and, gun drawn, crouched behind the open door.

"You folks need help?" a drawling voice called above the clatter of the engine.

Rachel struggled to hear the newcomer's words over the roaring pulse of fear beating in her ears.

"Tire's in a gully, and we're stuck," Stephen answered. "Can you pull us out?"

"Maybe," the voice said. "I'll have to take a look."

Metal ground against metal as gears wrenched and the approaching vehicle's engine halted. Clutching Jessica close, Rachel peered above the edge of the seat. A dark silhouette appeared before the headlights.

"Is it him?" she whispered to Stephen, "the gunman?"

Stephen held the Maglite out to the side, as he'd been FBI-trained in order not to present a ready target, and flipped on the beam.

A short, barrel-shaped man with a weather-beaten face blinked in the light. His hands dangled loosely at his sides, and his plaid flannel jacket was zipped tight over faded overalls. If he had a weapon, it wasn't visible. Or accessible. Stephen dipped the light lower. At the man's side trotted a magnificent German shepherd.

"I'm Clayton Jones," the newcomer called, "and this here is Rusty. But don't be scared. He looks mean, but he's gentle as a bunny rabbit."

Behind the open door Stephen holstered his gun, then stepped into the open and approached the farmer. Rachel watched, one arm around Jessica, the other hand grasping the butt of her automatic, ready to draw in an instant if trouble arose.

The stocky little man ambled to the front of the Explorer, squatted beside the left tire and studied the wheel and the terrain. His dog sat on the edge of the road beside him.

"Good thing I brought Betsy," Clayton Jones said.

"Betsy?" Stephen asked. "You said the dog's name is Rusty."

"It is." The farmer chuckled. "Betsy's over there. I've had her forty-five years, even longer than Sadie."

"Sadie?" Stephen said with a frown.

"Sadie's my wife. Betsy's my John Deere."

Stephen broke into a relieved grin and flashed Rachel an encouraging smile through the windshield. "You brought your tractor?"

Clayton stood and pushed back his sweat-stained, billed cap. "Saved me a trip back for her, didn't it?"

"You knew we were here?" Stephen said.

"I was watching your lights coming down the mountain. Saw 'em from the barnyard. When they stopped and switched off, I remembered this washed-out section of the old road from this past summer when we came berry picking up this way.'' He grinned and smacked his lips. ''Sadie makes the best blackberry jam in the valley. Anyways, I reckoned y'all were stuck, so I brung the tractor and a length of chain. Figured I'd pull you out afore you froze to death in the cold.''

''Mr. Jones,'' Stephen said, ''you are the answer to a prayer. Now, let me help you with that chain.''

Convinced of Clayton Jones's goodwill, Rachel climbed from the Explorer with Jessica in her arms and watched Stephen and the farmer attach a chain first to the vehicle and then to the ancient tractor. Rusty dogged his owner's footsteps like a black-and-tan shadow.

Clayton scampered onto the tractor seat with surprising alacrity for a man of his age and turned the starter. Clattering to life, Betsy belched foul-smelling smoke and began to move. Within minutes Clayton and Betsy had dragged the Explorer out of the gully onto solid ground.

''This road's clear straight down to the highway,'' he called over his shoulder, ''so you folks shouldn't have any problems from here on out.''

''We're very grateful for your help,'' Stephen said.

''Don't mention it,'' the cheerful little man said. ''That's why the good Lord put us on this earth, to help each other.'' He nodded at Rachel, his glance taking in the baby in her arms. ''Why don't you folks join us for supper? Sadie'll have it ready by the time we get there.''

"Thanks," Rachel said, "but we have people waiting for us, and we're late already."

"There's something else you can do to help." Stephen reached into his pocket, pulled out the thin leather folder that held his gold FBI shield and ID card, and showed them to Clayton. "I'm trying to get this woman and her child away from kidnappers who're after her. I'd appreciate it if you wouldn't mention to anyone that you've seen us."

"FBI, eh?" Clayton rubbed his chin and his blue eyes twinkled. "Be careful where you flash that badge in these hills, young feller. If som'un mistakes you for revenuers, you could be shot."

"Thanks for the tip," Stephen shook Clayton's hand. "And your help."

The farmer threw the tractor into gear and yelled above the clatter, "Follow me. I'll have you off the mountain in two shakes of a lamb's tail."

STEPHEN STOOD beneath the pulsing shower in the motel bathroom and let the rush of hot water pound the aches from his muscles. The firm twin bed in the other room beckoned. Even without remembering, he'd be willing to bet he'd never been so tired. And with good reason. Over thirty-six hours without sleep, a bullet wound in the arm and a knock on the head that had canceled his memories. Not to mention climbing down the side of one hell of a mountain.

He turned off the water and grinned to himself. As Jack used to say, at least it beat a sharp stick in the eye.

Where did that recollection come from? And who's Jack?

Bits and pieces of his memory were returning, as insubstantial—and as useless—as dust motes in sunlight. Why couldn't he remember the most important information, like who'd shot him? And why?

He grabbed a towel from the rack and rubbed the water from his body with a ferocity that made his skin tingle. He'd had his own score to settle before, but after he'd observed the pain and sorrow on Rachel's face as she watched the Kidbroughs drive away with Jessica, his determination to demand a payback from the scum who stalked them had doubled. In spades.

The jeans he'd taken from the cabin closet were a perfect fit. Either he and Uncle George were the same size, or Stephen had left clothes of his own in the closet. He ran his palm over his two-day stubble. Tomorrow he'd buy a razor. And a comb. He raked his fingers through his damp hair and grimaced at himself in the mirror when he noted the bullet wound blossoming like a pink rosebud on his bicep. It ached like the devil, but the pain was the least of his worries.

Thinking Rachel had already gone to sleep, he eased open the bathroom door and tiptoed into the main room, but both twin beds were empty. Only the dim light from the embers in the fireplace illuminated the room. Rachel stood in the shadows, gazing out the window at the darkness beyond.

The sight of her took his breath away.

Her thick, blond hair, drying into a mass of luxurious curls, cascaded across her shoulders. After her shower, she had donned one of the flannel shirts he'd filched from Uncle George's closet. With her arms crossed over her breasts, the shirt molded to the enticing curves of her bottom and exposed her legs, surprisingly long and coltish for a woman so petite. Pink, pearlized polish glistened on the nails of her bare feet.

In spite of his fatigue, hot, powerful desire spiked through him. With it came another memory. Rachel, asleep beside him, her magnificent hair fanned across the navy-blue pillowcases of his bed. Gripped by the intensity of the image, he started toward her, but common sense pulled him up short. That scene was no memory, but a figment of his own desire. Hadn't Rachel insisted they'd been just good friends? Like brother and sister, she'd said.

But the feelings he had for her didn't fit the situation she'd described. More than anything, he wanted to hold her—

Stop!

In disgust, he jammed his hands in the pockets of his jeans. He was married or, according to Rachel, at least engaged. In Atlanta, the woman to whom he'd pledged his love waited and worried. He couldn't allow himself to be caught up in the intimate circumstances of this situation and betray her.

When Rachel turned from the window, and he saw the tears tracking her cheeks, his good intentions vanished. In three quick strides he was beside her, drawing her into his arms, stroking her hair, whispering soft words of consolation, holding her against his heart.

She hadn't cried when Jessica left, and he had admired her stoicism. She must have known her tears would have frightened her daughter. Neither had Rachel cried on the short drive to Flat Rock, where they'd found the motel made up of tiny cabins and registered under the name of Mr. and Mrs. Clayton Jones. But now sobs racked her body as if her heart was breaking.

"She's so little," Rachel wept against his bare chest, "and she's never been away from me overnight. She won't understand why I've deserted her."

He tightened his arms around her and buried his face in her hair, fragrant with the scent of orange blossom shampoo. "She's safe. You have to keep reminding yourself of that. And the Kidbroughs will keep her happy."

"I know," she lifted her face to his and shot him a self-deprecating smile through her tears, "but *I'm* not happy. I miss her."

He couldn't help himself. Blaming the blow to his head, he lowered his lips to hers and kissed her as he'd wanted to since he'd first opened his eyes at his uncle's cabin. She tasted of salty tears and orange blossoms and a unique honeyed sweetness that sent his blood roaring through his veins.

She lifted her arms to his neck and strained on tiptoe against him, and he was only seconds from lifting her in his arms and carrying her to bed when she dropped her arms and pulled away.

Her green eyes were clouded and dazed as she stared up at him, breathless, with deep color staining her cheeks. "I don't think that kiss was a good idea."

He grinned sheepishly. "It seemed so, at the time."

She shook her head. "You were just feeling sorry for me."

"Yeah," he lied.

Sorry was the last thing he'd felt. But she was right. Getting emotionally involved wasn't a good idea, even if he didn't have a wife waiting at home. They needed to concentrate on finding the person who stalked them. Distractions, no matter how delicious, could get them both killed.

"We'd better get some sleep," he said, and silently cursed the huskiness that emotion had left in his voice. "We have work to do tomorrow."

"Okay." She avoided his eyes as she stepped around him and headed toward the twin bed farthest from the door.

He exerted all his self-control to keep from reaching for her again as she brushed past him.

"First thing tomorrow," he said, "we'll get some cash at an ATM. Credit cards would leave a trail our stalker could follow."

"Good idea," she murmured.

"That's assuming I have an ATM card." He took his wallet from the desk where he'd placed the contents from his pockets and rummaged through it. "Here it is."

When he yanked the ATM card from its slot, a folded piece of paper dropped to the floor. He retrieved it and smoothed it open on the desk.

"What is it?" Rachel asked.

"A drawing of a spiderweb. Why would I carry that in my wallet?"

She crossed the room to study the sketch. "It's a tattoo."

"A tattoo? Was I thinking of getting one?" The idea seemed foreign, but the drawing was familiar.

She shook her head. "You don't remember?"

A recollection flitted at the edge of his consciousness, but he couldn't grab it. "We've seen this before?"

Her face paled in the dim light. "In Savannah, on Margaret Maitland's kidnapper. And I have a feeling we're going to see it again."

Chapter Seven

"Does this spiderweb tattoo have special significance?" Stephen asked.

"It's a badge of honor among white hate groups," Rachel said. "A member isn't entitled to wear it until he's killed for the cause."

"Nice guys," he said with a grimace. "Did we ever work a case involving these creeps?"

"Besides the Maitland kidnapping?" She curled her legs beneath her, settled on the bed and wrinkled her forehead in thought. "Only one, that I can remember. A bank robbery a few years back."

"You'll have to fill me in," he snapped, frustrated by his lack of recall—and the resurgence of his desire at the sight of her, nestled atop the covers in her too-big shirt, wide-eyed, with her magnificent hair in disarray.

"We had an added incentive to catch these guys," she explained. "Not only did they shoot a bank security guard, they battered an elderly woman."

"But we *did* catch them?"

She nodded. "Their take was less than three thousand dollars. When we arrested them, they claimed they'd stolen the money to finance their cause but in the few days it took us to catch up with them, they managed to spend it all. Cigarettes, beer and lottery tickets. Some cause, huh?''

''Could those two be the ones after us?''

''Not likely.'' She stifled a yawn with her hand. ''One was killed in a prison brawl shortly after sentencing. The other will be locked up for a long time.''

''And their fellow hatemongers?''

''From what our investigation revealed, they were a loosely organized group without significant goals, except for weekly beer busts and late-night rides through town looking for non-Caucasian victims to bash.''

He settled into a chair by the fire and stared at the drawing in his hand, attempting through the force of his will to recapture his memories.

His only result was a headache.

''Why is this sketch in my wallet?'' he muttered, and rubbed his throbbing temples. ''Have I carried it since the Maitland case?''

She shook her head. ''The paper looks too new, and its creases aren't worn enough to be that old.''

''If the paper's new, this tattoo could be connected to a recent case I was following and totally unrelated to whoever's after us.''

''We won't figure that out tonight.'' Her soft, empathetic smile made him want to kiss her again. ''You need sleep.''

Fatigue dragged at him, quenching his desire. ''I can't argue with that.''

"Who knows? Maybe you'll have your memory back when you wake up." She scooted under the covers and snuggled into her pillow. "Sleep well."

He turned out the light, but the rest he needed so desperately didn't come. He lay for what seemed like hours, listening to the soft sounds of her breathing before he drifted into sleep.

RACHEL AWAKENED to the welcoming aroma of fresh-brewed coffee, but as memories of the past twenty-four hours flooded her, she buried deeper in the bed and yanked the covers over her head.

Jessica's absence burned like a raw wound in her heart, and she silently cursed the circumstances that separated her from her daughter.

In addition to the pain of missing her child, Rachel suffered the embarrassment of having surrendered to her emotions the previous night. Last night she'd been too tired to feel ashamed. After a good night's sleep, mortification reared its ugly head. She must have been temporarily insane to have kissed Stephen that way. And she'd had to employ every ounce of self-control to break away.

She groaned and burrowed deeper under the blankets. No longer could she kid herself, insisting that she considered Stephen only a friend. Just the thought of him, lying asleep in the bed next to hers, sent her pulse into overdrive and made breathing a chore.

Sure, he'd kissed her first, but she couldn't blame him for that. After all, hadn't he admitted she was the only person who seemed familiar? Wasn't she the one who'd burst into tears over missing Jess? He was just being comforting, while she'd been a shameless dim-wit.

She moaned with chagrin. As soon as his memories returned, he would remember his wife in Atlanta, feel really embarrassed over his behavior last night—and perhaps even blame Rachel for leading him on.

And she would end up looking like a chump.

She pounded her pillow with her fists, more desperate now than ever to discover who stalked them, so she could return to Jessica and get away from Stephen.

Before she made a fool of herself. Again.

"Rachel?" Stephen tugged at the covers. "You awake?"

She gripped the blankets tighter over her head. "Go away."

Her face burned over how brazenly she'd returned his kiss last night. She couldn't face him. Not yet.

"You were moaning. You okay?"

"Just dandy," she muttered with another groan and squirmed deeper into the bed.

"You sure you're not ill?"

The man might have lost his memory, but his persistence was operating on all cylinders. "I'm fine. Please, leave me alone."

"Breakfast is ready." He jerked the covers again.

"I'm not hungry."

"Good. That leaves more for me. I don't remember, of course, but I doubt you like blueberry muffins or three-cheese omelets."

Her stomach growled with hunger. She hadn't eaten since lunch yesterday. Even though the Kidbroughs had ordered supper for her at the restaurant last night, she'd been too distraught over saying good-bye to Jessica to eat.

With the suddenness of an explosion and the clarity of a spring day, an answer to her problem hit her. She would explain her plan to Stephen over breakfast. As long as she concentrated on getting home, she wouldn't be distracted by him.

She rolled the covers off her face and came eye-to-eye with Stephen, sitting on the edge of her bed and looking very pleased with himself.

"Where'd you find breakfast?" she asked.

"The motel has a great little mom-and-pop restaurant. And they deliver."

He stood and indicated the small table he'd moved in front of the fireplace, where a cheerful fire crackled. Sunlight tumbled through the windows at an angle that told her she'd slept until mid-morning. The cabin was redolent with the smell of burning hickory logs, strong coffee and hot, buttery bread.

Even more appealing than breakfast was Stephen. He wore tight jeans, a hunter-green plaid shirt that brought out emerald highlights in his dark brown eyes, and sturdy work boots, an attractive alternative to his suit-and-tie FBI uniform.

A three-day beard that would make lesser men appear scruffy gave him a rugged and rakish appearance. She was relieved to notice his color was better and the tight lines around his eyes had eased. The night's rest had done him good.

"Well?" He was appraising her with a quizzical tilt of his head.

Blushing at being caught daydreaming, she fumbled for something to say. "Maybe I am a *little* hungry."

She tossed back the covers, forgetting until that moment that she wore only a flannel shirt that barely reached her thighs. With a desperate lunge, she whipped the top blanket off the bed and wrapped it around her.

Stephen crossed to the table and pulled out a chair.

Attempting to regain her dignity, she kicked the trailing blanket away from her feet, strode to the table and sat. Stephen leaned over her from behind and poured her coffee.

The scent of him, soapy fresh but unmistakably masculine, almost made her forget her plan. She took a long sip of the hot, fortifying brew and plunged ahead before he could distract her again. "I've decided what we have to do."

"You have?" He took a chair across from her, poured himself a cup, and confronted her with raised eyebrows over the rim. "And what did you decide?"

"We contact your Atlanta office."

"And?"

"Ask for your partner."

"Then what?"

"We explain about your amnesia and the person who's stalking us and ask to be sequestered in an FBI safe house until the Bureau can locate and capture the people who're after us." She sat back in her chair, pleased with her strategy and wondering why she hadn't thought of it sooner.

Stephen continued to stare at her over his coffee cup, but he didn't say a word.

"Well?" she demanded. "What do you think?"

He set his cup in its saucer, reached across the table for her hand, and entwined his fingers with hers before she could pull away. "That's exactly what we're expected to do."

"So?"

"So maybe whoever's after us is watching the office and my partner, even tapping his phone." Stephen theorized, "and what if more than one man is after us?" He nodded toward the dresser where the sketch of the tattoo lay. "What if an entire group of white supremacists are on our trail?"

Rachel ducked her head over her breakfast to hide her heated face. Stephen had not only stirred her senses, he'd obviously scrambled her brains. She should have factored in the possibility of more than one stalker. Drawing a deep breath, she concentrated on the problem that faced them and was immediately aware of a niggling inconsistency.

"When you first called to warn me," she reminded him, "you said the threat concerned a case we worked in Savannah. But the only two cases involving members of hate groups are that bank robbery and the Maitland kidnapping."

"The only two that we know of," he amended.

"Right. And of those two, one of the bank robbers is dead, the other locked away. And Jason Bender shot and killed both the Maitland kidnappers."

"Could be the surviving bank robber or the kidnappers— What were their names?"

"Bubba and Weed," she said.

"Could be the bank robber or Bubba and Weed have friends or relatives who are out for revenge?"

"If it's revenge for Bubba and Weed, why go after us?" she asked. "Jason shot them."

Their glances met over the table. Stephen apparently had the same thought.

"Contact Jason," he said. "See if he's had any threats."

Rachel managed to reach the phone on the dresser without stumbling over her blanket and dialed the Savannah office of the FBI. Marie, the same receptionist who'd worked there when Rachel left, answered.

"Sorry, Rache," she said when Rachel had identified herself and asked for Jason, "Jason left a few days ago for a few weeks' vacation."

"Did he leave a number where he can be reached?"

"He's hiking the Appalachian trail, so he's incommunicado, except for every few days, when he checks in for his messages. Do you want to leave one?"

"No," Rachel said, thinking quickly, "but could you tell me if anyone else has called for him?"

"It's been like old home week around here," Marie said. "Just after Jason left, Stephen Chandler called, looking for him."

"Thanks, Marie."

Rachel hung up the phone and repeated Marie's words to Stephen.

"If I called Jason to warn him," Stephen said, "then we're on the right track with the hate group."

Rachel shrugged. "Maybe. Or you could have been

calling about an entirely different case, and the timing is just coincidental. I still think we should go to Atlanta and ask the Bureau for help.''

Stephen frowned. ''My gut says no.''

Rachel slid back into her chair. ''You're not suggesting the Bureau's after us?''

He shook his head. ''I don't know what to think. All I know is that every time you mention contacting the FBI, alarms go off in my head.''

She had too much respect for his instincts to argue. ''So what do we do now?''

''Finish your breakfast,'' he said with a devilish grin. ''Who knows when we'll have a chance to eat again?''

She dug into her omelet, but barely tasted it. How had she landed in such a mess? On the run from a nameless, faceless killer, separated from her child, and too enticingly close to another woman's husband—who just happened to be the father of her baby.

Her glance darted around the tiny room in an attempt to avoid meeting Stephen's gaze, and her attention fell on Stephen's computer case.

''You used to keep a daily journal,'' she said. ''Maybe the answers we need are in your computer.''

An hour later she wished she'd never mentioned his computer. They'd learned his files were password-protected, and without FBI decrypting software, they hadn't a prayer of determining what that password was, regardless of how many key words or word-numeral combinations they tried. Stephen had known enough about circumventing passwords to make his unbreakable.

"I give up," Stephen finally admitted. "Looks like returning to Atlanta is our only choice."

She felt her eyes widen with surprise. "You're ready to ask the Bureau for help?"

He shook his head. "I want to try retracing my movements of the last few days. I must have stumbled onto something that made me warn you. We have to figure out what that was, and we'll never do it from here."

"But you'll be recognized in Atlanta."

"Not if I make some changes," he said with a twinkle in his eye. "And you, too."

"Me?"

"You're coming with me. I'll need your help."

Rachel started to protest, but realized she had little choice. She couldn't return to Jessica or her work until their stalkers were captured. And she couldn't leave Stephen to operate on his own, without memories. Besides, they worked well as partners. Their individual investigative techniques complemented each other's, and they'd solve this case faster together.

The sooner it was solved, the sooner she could walk out of Stephen's life. The prospect gave her relief, but no pleasure.

"You'll need clothes," he said.

She couldn't argue with that. She'd washed her underwear before going to bed last night, so it had been fresh and dry this morning, but her blouse was getting a bit dingy, and her slacks looked as if she'd slept in them.

"You'll also need a disguise," he added. "And we

should change vehicles. That makes cash our first necessity. Do you have any?''

''Sorry.'' A flush of embarrassment worked its way up her cheeks. Since quitting her well-paying job as an agent, money had been a continual problem. She doubted she had more than fifty dollars in her wallet, and not much more in her checking account, at least till payday.

Stephen shrugged and chuckled. ''We know enough about robbing banks—''

''That's not funny. What about the ATM card you found last night?''

''An ATM withdrawal would be the quickest way, and the least likely to attract attention, but my card's useless without my personal identification number.''

''Which you can't remember.''

''Right.'' His expression was rueful.

''It's probably in your computer,'' she said with a scowl of frustration.

''My checkbook was in my computer case. I can cash a check at the branch bank we passed after leaving Shoney's last night.''

Her medical school training kicked in as she noted Stephen's diminished color, the returning pain lines around his eyes, and the fatigue in his voice. He shouldn't be going anywhere, not for a while.

''Let me cash the check and take care of the car while you stay here and rest.''

''I *can't* rest.'' His eyes flashed with anger, and he clenched his fingers into fists. ''Operating in the dark like this is driving me crazy.''

''You'll be in better shape to investigate in Atlanta

if you pamper that arm now.'' She had checked his wound after breakfast and been glad to discover no signs of infection. However, he'd still lost a lot of blood and he needed time to recuperate. Pushing himself to the limits of his endurance was only asking for trouble. "We'll make a list of everything we need. While I shop, you rest—"

He scowled and shook his head.

"Then spend the time trying to crack your computer password," she suggested gently. "Without it, you can't even access your e-mail."

His expression softened, and she had to look away from the warmth in his eyes.

"You're pretty special, Doc. How did I ever let a partner like you get away?"

"I was no match for a promotion and big pay raise. Now, will you help me make a list?"

SHE HAD USED most of the day to find what she needed. First, long lines at the bank delayed her when she cashed Stephen's check. Finding a garage that would store her Explorer out of sight had taken even longer. But what had exhausted her most was trying not to call attention to herself by glancing over her shoulder every few minutes to see if someone was watching her. Out in the open she'd felt exposed, vulnerable and frightened.

By the time she'd purchased all the items on the list she and Stephen had compiled, the late-afternoon sun was sinking over Mount Pisgah.

She drove the rented Blazer into the parking place in front of their cabin and was removing several bags and packages from the back when the front door banged open. Startled, she dropped the parcels and reached for her gun. She stopped herself from drawing when she saw Stephen bounding down the steps.

"You were gone so long," he said, "I was worried. Thank God, you're safe."

She gathered her packages again and slammed the rear hatch. "The streets and stores are clogged with tourist traffic. Everyone comes to the mountains for the fall foliage."

"Let me help." He tried to take some of the packages from her.

"I have them." She hurried inside, and Stephen followed.

After dumping her bundles on the nearest bed, she collapsed in a chair in front of the fire. "I hate shopping."

Stephen began unpacking items from the bags. "I thought women lived to shop."

"Not this one. I don't care if I never see the inside of a store again." She grinned to take the edge off her complaint. "Maybe I'm missing an essential female gene."

He raised his eyebrows and lifted his lips in a slow smile. "From where I'm standing, I'd say you're well equipped with everything essentially female."

"Remember you're a married man, Chandler. That knock on the head must have affected more than your memories."

Her teasing reprimand served its purpose. His heated look dissolved into an expression of chagrin.

She closed her eyes and sighed. His earlier appreciative glance had given *cabin fever* an entirely new meaning. For two cents, she would load everything back into the Blazer so they could take off for Atlanta immediately, and she could avoid another intimate night in the motel, but her medical expertise reminded her that Stephen needed another good night's rest to recuperate.

She doubted *she'd* sleep well. Besides missing Jessica and worrying about who was stalking them, she'd become too aware of Stephen and the response he evoked in her. The prospect of spending another night in the same room with him made her uncomfortable.

To save herself from further scrutiny by Stephen, she waved a hand at the packages on the bed. ''Do you think these disguises will work?''

He hunched his shoulders. ''They'll keep a casual observer from spotting us and passing that information on. That's the most we can hope for.''

She nodded. They wouldn't be in disguise long. She couldn't continue living like this—afraid for her life, missing her child and tormented by the proximity of the man she loved but could never have. If their attempt to reconstruct Stephen's actions his last few days in Atlanta didn't yield their stalkers' identities, they'd be out of options.

If that happened, she'd go to the FBI office in Atlanta and ask for help.

No matter what Stephen said.

Chapter Eight

The patter of drizzling rain against the window beside his bed awoke Stephen before daybreak. For the first time since he'd regained consciousness in his uncle's cabin, he felt rested. Flexing his wounded arm gingerly, he detected only a slight ache, a tribute to Rachel's first aid skill.

He raised himself on his elbows and gazed at the woman asleep in the other bed. Several times during the night he had awakened to hear her turning, tossing and occasionally moaning softly in her dreams, so he doubted she'd slept well. Who could blame her, with a killer on her trail and her tiny daughter so far away?

More than once he'd been tempted to go to her, to slip beneath the covers and hold her close until she slept soundly, but he'd known he couldn't trust his responses at that proximity.

Besides, according to Rachel, he was *married,* damn it. If only he could remember his wife, perhaps his powerful attraction to Rachel would disappear.

With difficulty he shoved his fascination with his former partner to the back of his mind. More important than the emotions she stirred in him was catching the people who pursued them. Then he and Rachel could return to their normal lives and routines.

He considered again her continued insistence that they call his partner at the Atlanta office, but, despite the logic of her suggestion, he couldn't risk making contact. He had lost his memories, but his instincts remained strong, warning him that danger lay down that path.

Moving quietly to keep from waking her, he threw back the covers. Before pulling on his jeans, he wrapped his right knee with an Ace bandage to hold it rigid. His resulting stiff-legged gait and the accompanying cane would be part of his disguise. Favoring his wounded arm, he tugged on a black turtleneck sweater and zipped his jeans.

In the cabin's bathroom, he liberally streaked gray dye through his sideburns, the dark hair at his temples, and his growing beard. Round gold-rimmed glasses with rose-colored lenses completed his camouflage. The disguise wouldn't fool anyone who knew him, but it might throw off someone looking for a clean-cut FBI agent.

When he stepped out of the bathroom, he discovered Rachel, awake and dressed, packing a soft-sided suitcase she'd purchased the day before.

Last night she had cropped her blond hair to just below her ears and colored it a rich auburn. The new hue emphasized the startling green of her eyes. This morning, through the skillful application of makeup, a smattering of becoming freckles decorated her nose and cheeks. She had exchanged her tailored slacks and sweater for black tights, black patent-leather Doc Martens and a brilliant red bulky pullover sweater that covered her trim thighs. Gigantic medallions of filigreed silver dangled from her ears.

"What do you think?" She pirouetted in front of him.

"You have great taste," he teased. "You auditioning to join the Spice Girls?"

She wrinkled her nose in a manner that jolted his senses. "I chose everything I ordinarily would *not* buy."

"It works. Your own mother probably wouldn't recognize you."

"You and I make quite a pair, huh?" Her dazzling smile threatened to dissolve all his good intentions to keep his distance.

"Do you want to order breakfast in the room," he asked, "or hit the road?"

"This rain will slow us down. Let's get started, as soon as I've called the Kidbroughs to check on Jessica."

Loading their scant belongings into the Blazer took only a few minutes. After a stop at the motel office to settle their bill, they turned onto rain-slicked Highway 64 and headed west.

In the darkness of the predawn morning, neither noticed the navy blue sedan as it pulled out from behind the nearest cabin without its headlights and followed them onto the highway at a distance.

AT CASHIERS Rachel turned south on Highway 27, a narrow winding road that would take them out of the mountains to the interstate.

The wipers swept steady rain from the windshield with a hypnotic rhythm, and she had to keep talking to prevent herself from falling asleep. "Did you have any luck getting into your computer while I was shopping yesterday?"

"No. But I made a few phone calls that narrowed our search."

"What kind of calls?"

She glanced at him in alarm, then returned her attention to the treacherous, curving road and shifted the Blazer into low gear for the steep descent.

"I called the federal penitentiary where Johnny Slade is jailed and talked to the warden. I wanted to find out whether Johnny has been in touch recently with any wise guys from the mob."

"What did you find out?"

"We can scratch Johnny Slade from our list of probable suspects."

"Why?"

"He's been in the prison infirmary for the past three months, dying of lung cancer."

"If he's dying in prison, doesn't that give him a greater motive to kill us? After all, we put him there."

"That was my first reaction. But the warden assures me that Slade hasn't had any visitors."

"Not even family?"

"No one."

Sympathy for Slade stabbed through her. She remembered him as a cocky, arrogant con man, a flashy dresser with an eye for women and a glib tongue.

She'd disliked him instantly the first time she met him, but even so, he didn't deserve to die alone. "No letters, phone calls?"

"Nothing. So unless some friend or relative is acting on his own for Johnny's revenge—"

"That's doubtful, isn't it, since no one even bothers to visit when he's dying?"

"That brings us back to the hate group."

She sighed. "And a dead end."

"A poor choice of words," he said with a wry grimace.

She glanced in the rearview mirror. Unable to pass on the narrow, two-lane road, cars and trucks had stacked up behind them.

"In this kind of traffic," she said, "we can't tell whether we're being followed."

"How could anyone be tailing us, unless they picked up our trail at the motel? And if they had, I doubt we'd be here now to talk about it."

An hour later they left the mountains and entered the rolling piedmont. In a quaint little town named Walhalla that historical markers claimed was founded by German immigrants, they stopped for breakfast.

A few miles outside Walhalla, they picked up I-85 and headed southwest toward Atlanta. In bumper-to-bumper, six-lane traffic, Rachel felt anonymous for the first time since leaving George Windham's cabin. With their disguises and rented sport utility vehicle, they'd be hard to recognize.

Exiting onto I-285 that circled Atlanta, she headed toward the suburb listed on Stephen's driver's license. They planned to search his place first. Rachel hoped he'd sent his wife into hiding before leaving Atlanta, not only for the woman's safety but also because Rachel wasn't looking forward to meeting the ex-beauty queen and advertising executive Stephen had married.

Not that she was jealous, she assured herself.

Yeah, right.

When they reached the bedroom community listed on Stephen's driver's license, they stopped and asked a letter carrier for directions to the street where Stephen lived. The address turned out to be a group of large apartment buildings, not unlike the complex where Stephen had rented in Savannah.

Looking for signs of surveillance, Rachel circled Stephen's apartment building several times. Most of the parking spaces were vacant, their occupants probably at work for the day. The few cars remaining were empty.

"The building has a single main entrance," Stephen noted. "If anyone sees us going inside, they won't be able to tell which apartment we're visiting."

Rachel pulled into a parking space marked Visitors. "Do you have your gun?"

He opened his jacket to reveal his shoulder holster. "And you?"

She reached into the back seat for an oversize purse with a shoulder strap. "It's here. Ready?"

They climbed out of the vehicle and started up the tiered walkway that led to the entrance. The air, while cool, was several degrees warmer than the mountains had been, and the surrounding trees hadn't surrendered yet to autumn's colorful palette. All that greenery offered a hundred places for an assassin to hide, but not a branch or leaf stirred in the midday stillness.

Rachel stopped and scanned the complex, checking doors and windows for signs of anyone watching. Not a curtain moved. She turned and followed Stephen, whose bound knee slowed his progress up the stairs.

"If I was staking out this place," she said, "I'd plant a lookout in the lobby."

"If a lookout's waiting, our disguises will give us the element of surprise."

"I hope so," she said doubtfully.

He swung open the double glass doors, and Rachel, her right hand grasping the gun inside her purse, entered the lobby first. The room was deserted, its only sound piped-in, easy-listening music. A discreet sign opposite the tenants' mailboxes indicated which apartment numbers could be accessed from which hallway. Stephen's apartment was to the left.

Stephen motioned Rachel behind him and proceded down the dimly lit hall. They weren't out of danger yet. The most obvious place a killer might be waiting was inside Stephen's apartment.

When they reached his apartment, they drew their guns. Standing to the side of the entrance with Rachel backed against the wall on the opposite side, Stephen tried the door.

It was unlocked.

With a quick flick of his wrist, he flung the door open and waited.

Not a sound issued from inside the apartment.

Stephen leaned into the doorway for a split-second glance and just as quickly withdrew. Rachel raised her eyebrows in question, and he shook his head. He hadn't spotted anyone.

But that didn't mean no one was there.

Rachel followed Stephen inside. A tiny foyer led into an open floor plan, and she could observe the living and dining areas and kitchen from where she stood. The rooms were deserted.

Except for the mess.

Cushions had been tossed from sofas and chairs and ripped apart. The kitchen cabinets—even the refrigerator—stood open, and dishes had been smashed on the ceramic tile floor. Mirrors were shattered, littering the floor with shards of glass. Contents of drawers and bookcases had been scattered across the living room carpeting. Even potted plants had been uprooted from their containers and their dirt strewn across the floor.

Someone had searched the apartment, but not with the rational calm of a professional. The stench of out-of-control anger and desperation hung in the air.

Stephen touched her arm and pointed to the foot of the stairs in the foyer. Moving silently, he headed up them, weapon at the ready. She followed, guarding his back.

The stairs led to a master suite on the second floor that had suffered the same mistreatment as the rooms below. Linens had been torn from the bed, clothes dumped from the closets, and the pillows and mattress cover ripped apart.

"What were they looking for?" Rachel whispered for the first time since entering the apartment.

"Me," Stephen said with a grimace. "And they

were obviously mad as hell when they didn't find me.''

Rachel shoved her gun into her purse and placed it on the dresser. ''We have our own search to conduct.''

Holstering his weapon, Stephen surveyed the trashed room with a shake of his head. ''You really think we'll find anything in all this mess?''

''Won't know till we try.''

She leaned down and picked up a framed picture from the floor where it had apparently landed after being knocked from the dresser. In spite of the cracked glass, she recognized immediately the snapshot Jason Bender had taken of her and Stephen the night of his going-away party. They were smiling at each other, oblivious of the camera, and the warmth in their expressions left little to the imagination.

Rachel frowned. Stephen's wife must have *loved* having that photo prominently displayed in her bedroom.

''You said I was married.'' Stephen's accusing tone interrupted her thoughts.

''What?''

''Only men's clothing is here. If I have a wife, where are her belongings?''

''She must have taken them with her when she went into hiding.''

''Everything?'' Stephen's expression was skeptical. He stepped into the adjacent bathroom and returned in a few seconds. ''She didn't leave so much as a tube of lipstick or an old bathrobe. If she went into hiding in a hurry, why did she take time to clean out every trace?''

''Maybe the wedding hasn't taken place yet.'' Joy shot through her at the possibility—and just as quickly died. Just because Stephen hadn't married his beauty queen yet, didn't mean he wouldn't be. And soon.

''Why don't I at least have a picture of her? Is that what you're holding?''

Rachel placed the photo facedown on the dresser. ''It's just an old snapshot from your days in Savannah.''

''Let me see.''

Reluctantly she handed him the frame.

When he looked at the picture, he lifted his eyebrows in twin peaks of surprise and turned his amazed look on Rachel. Her face flamed with embarrassment.

''You told me we were just friends.'' Accusation edged his words and he shook the framed photo at her. ''Like brother and sister, you said.''

''That's right,'' she insisted.

He narrowed his eyes. ''Brothers and sisters don't look at each other like this.''

She scrambled for an explanation. ''It was a party. We'd had too much to drink.''

''You don't look drunk.''

''Really,'' she said nervously, ''you're reading something into the photograph that isn't there.''

''Yeah?'' His dark-eyed gaze bore into her. ''Then why did I keep *this* picture on my dresser?''

She wished she knew. ''As a joke?''

''This isn't funny, Doc.''

"We don't know that you kept it on the dresser. Whoever vandalized this place could have found it in the bottom of a drawer and tossed it out."

He shook his head, as if uncertain whether to accept her explanation, and riveted her with piercing stare. "How can I be sure you're being straight with me?"

"You can't." She forced herself to meet his gaze without flinching. "But you have to realize that if I intended to harm you, I've had ample opportunities and used none."

She sank onto the edge of the bed to stop her knees from trembling.

Confusion clouded his eyes, but the iron set of his jaw didn't soften. "For all I know, you could be leading me into some kind of trap."

"What?" His accusation stung her.

"You just haven't sprung it yet."

"If you really believe that, there's the phone." She nodded toward the bedside table. "Call the Atlanta FBI office. Have *them* help you."

His dark eyes glinted with bewilderment. "My instincts tell me not to call in the FBI. But they also warn me you're not telling the whole truth."

Oh boy, he had that right.

She wasn't about to share her feelings for him. Or reveal that he was Jessica's father. But she had to convince him she was on his side or he might go charging off, straight into danger, without the memories he needed to keep him safe.

"Look," she said in her most reasonable tone, "*you* called me, *you* faxed me the map to the cabin, *you're* the one who won't let me go to the authorities for help, and *you* can't tell me who's after us. If anyone has a right to be wary, it should be me.''

He grabbed her by her shoulders, hauled her to her feet and lowered his face only inches from hers. ''What aren't you telling me?''

His grip was firm and not uncomfortable, but she found breathing difficult with him so near. She closed her eyes against the magnificence of his anger. ''If I misled you about your marital state, I apologize. If you remember, I said from the beginning I'd heard only rumors. I never claimed to know the gospel truth.''

He released her and stepped away, and, in spite of his annoyance with her, she wished him close again.

''I'm sorry.'' He raked his fingers through his hair in frustration. ''The tension is getting to me, or I wouldn't have questioned your motives.''

''Forget it,'' she said, relief cascading through her.

He surveyed the room and shook his head. ''Things just don't add up somehow.''

''This apartment may not be what it seems,'' she suggested. ''Some agents keep a separate residence that they list on public documents to protect the privacy of their families. You could be married. We just don't know where Anne Michelle lives.''

He surveyed the contents of the closet scattered across the floor. ''Seems like too many clothes here for a second residence.''

He was right, but she couldn't allow herself to accept that he wasn't married. That belief stirred up too many dangerous emotions, and she needed a clear mind, unencumbered by sentiment. "If your wedding was recent, you may not have moved all your clothes out yet."

His expression turned thoughtful. "If you're right, the location of that other residence may be what our intruder was after, thinking that's where I'm hiding."

"There's one way to find out. Let's see if we can locate an address book. You search here. I'll check the first floor." She hastened downstairs to escape those familiar navy blue sheets and the unsettling memories they generated.

The sooner she found evidence of who pursued them, the sooner she could escape the exquisite torture of Stephen's presence. Being with him the past few days had brought back with startling clarity how much she'd missed him, how much she had longed to share his daughter with him.

And how hard she'd tried to convince herself he'd been only a good friend.

She knelt beside a jumble of papers on the living room rug and began sorting. No point now in admitting how much she loved him. As soon as his memories returned, he'd go back to Anne Michelle.

Ignoring the jealousy raging within her, Rachel pawed through piles of bill receipts, appliance warranties and old programs from Atlanta Braves games, but she could find no trace of an address book. Not even a Christmas card list.

She flipped through books as she replaced them on their shelves, including a complete collection of the novels of Scott Turow and John Grisham, and John Douglas's *Mindhunter,* relating his experiences as an

FBI profiler, but she discovered nothing to indicate anything significant about Stephen's life in Atlanta.

And no hint of who might be after them.

She had practically given up when she spotted a tiny corner of paper visible beneath the edge of the upholstered sofa skirt. Retrieving it, she found Anne Michelle Logan's name etched in burgundy ink on a pale pink business card with the logo and downtown Atlanta address of Creative Marketing, where Stephen's fiancée was an account executive.

Rachel started to call to Stephen, still upstairs, then changed her mind. Showing his face in Atlanta was too dangerous, even in disguise, but Rachel wasn't known in the city. She could easily visit Anne Michelle's office and find out whether the woman had been to work the past few days. If she could track Anne Michelle, Rachel might be able to discover who was stalking her and Stephen.

A shudder racked her. If Rachel could find Anne Michelle, so could the man who had shot Stephen. She wondered if Anne Michelle was still alive.

"Any luck, Doc?" Stephen called from the bottom of the stairs.

She shook her head and hid Anne Michelle's card in her palm. "I didn't find anything useful. And if the intruders found anything, like an address book, they took it with them. What about you?"

"Upstairs is clean," he flashed a familiar grin that made her heart ache, "in a manner of speaking."

"So we've hit another dead end."

"Not exactly. I have an idea."

Stephen's ideas were legendary. Her skill was analyzing and interpreting hard evidence, but Stephen's speciality was ferreting out information, often in ways no one else would have thought of.

"I'm listening," she said.

"We check into a downtown hotel—"

"You're not serious? What if somebody recognizes you?"

"I checked the Yellow Pages upstairs. There's a privately owned hotel on Peachtree Street a few blocks from downtown. The Sidney Lanier. Their ad touts 'privacy, peacefulness and discretion.'"

"Okay, for the sake of discussion, we check into the Lanier. Then what?"

"I request two weeks' back issues of the *Atlanta Constitution*," he said.

"You think our spider-tattoo hate group might have had some recent press?"

"The newspapers are as good a place to start as any."

The corner of the business card cut into her hand, reminding Rachel that Anne Michelle's office was on Peachtree Street. If they stayed at the Lanier, while Stephen studied back issues of the papers, Rachel could do some snooping on her own.

"Okay," she said. "Anything you want to take with you from here?"

"Wearing my own clothes probably isn't a good idea." He rubbed the stubble on his cheek. "And I won't be needing my shaving kit."

She ran upstairs for her purse, shoved the business card into an inside pocket and joined Stephen downstairs.

Minutes later, they were headed for downtown Atlanta in the rented Blazer. Traffic on the interstate bypass was heavy, and Rachel stayed alert for signs directing her to downtown. Stephen kept his attention on the rearview mirrors.

"Anybody following us?" she asked.

"Besides several thousand commuters on their way home from work?" he asked with a wry grimace. "Hard to tell. There's a dark blue sedan that looks familiar a few car lengths back, but in this jam, I can't tell whether it's on our tail or just caught in traffic."

Rachel took the exit for downtown, and the blue sedan followed. Along with a few hundred other vehicles. Ahead of them the Atlanta skyline with its impressive gold-domed capitol building stood silhouetted against the afternoon sun.

Soon they were traveling a one-way street between the city's skyscrapers.

"Turn here," Stephen directed.

Rachel maneuvered the turn onto Peachtree Street. "Is that sedan still behind us?"

Stephen craned his neck and observed over the rear seat. "Looks like it."

"Coincidence?"

"I don't believe in coincidence." He faced the front and peered through the windshield. "There's the entrance to the Sidney Lanier. Turn in that store lot across the street and park, and we'll see what the blue car does."

Rachel whipped into the parking lot opposite the hotel and pulled into an empty space.

The blue sedan shot straight past without slowing. She shut off the engine, but made no move to get out of the car. She'd done surveillance too many times to be convinced by the car's disappearance that it hadn't been on their tail. If it was trailing them, the driver would circle the block, giving them time to go inside before he returned and parked where he could watch their car.

"How long should we wait?" she asked Stephen.

He unhooked his seat belt and settled back in his seat. "If they're not back in thirty minutes, we'll check into the hotel. If that car passes again, we'll have to shake them and look for another place to stay."

For almost forty-five minutes, they watched the street. When they caught no sign of the dark blue sedan again, they drove across to the hotel lot, retrieved their luggage from the back of the blazer and entered the hotel.

Neither of them had noticed a man in a brown leather jacket, hidden in a viburnum hedge half a block down the street, who observed them as intently as they surveyed the passing traffic.

When Rachel and Stephen entered the hotel with their luggage, he ground out the cigarette he'd been smoking and sprinted a half block to the dark blue sedan, parked out of sight of the hotel entrance.

"Did they check in?" the man behind the wheel asked the observer.

"Yeah, luggage and all."

"Do we take 'em now?"

The man in the bomber jacket shook his head. "Not yet."

"So what do we do?"

"We wait."

Chapter Nine

Stephen surveyed the small but elegant lobby. At the far end of the room an elderly couple sat before a crackling fire in wing chairs upholstered in needlepoint. Paintings of English landscapes and hunting scenes graced the muted walls, rich oriental rugs provided a splash of color on the gleaming hardwood floor, and arrangements of fall flowers had been placed on every surface. Polished brass, sparkling mullioned windows, and a pervasive hint of lemon oil testified to the hotel's immaculate housekeeping.

"Nice," Rachel murmured beside him.

"Do me a favor," he said. "Wait here in the lobby a few minutes."

Her deep green eyes widened in alarm. "What are you going to do?"

"Find us a room. It won't take long."

"You won't leave the hotel?"

He shook his head.

"Okay." Her expression still puzzled, she crossed the lobby, settled on a camelback sofa in front of a spacious bay window and picked up a copy of *Southern Living* from the coffee table.

Stephen approached the registration desk.

"May I help you, sir?" the young female clerk behind the desk asked in a quiet, cultured drawl.

He cast a glance over his shoulder at Rachel, who raised her gaze from the magazine and flashed him a quizzical smile. Turning back to the clerk with what he hoped was an ingratiating smile, he leaned over the counter and whispered, "My wife is terrified of being caught in a hotel fire. Do you have a suite on the first floor?"

The clerk's ready smile dissolved. "I'm sorry, sir, but only our restaurant, gift shop and conference rooms occupy the first floor." Her expression brightened. "But I have a suite on the third floor that might suit your needs. Would you like to see it?"

"Please."

She rang a silver bell, and at its discreet chime, an elderly black bellman appeared. She reached into a cubbyhole behind the desk and extracted a key. "Josiah, show this gentleman to Suite 345, and be sure to point out the fire escape."

"This way, sir."

Stephen followed the tall, rake-thin man to a bank of elevator doors. Before Josiah could push the up button, Stephen asked, "Mind if we use the stairs?"

"Whatever you say, sir."

Josiah turned to the right and ambled down a wide corridor and Stephen followed, taking in every possible exit. They passed a glass-fronted restaurant and several shops before reaching the stairwell at the end of the hall. Josiah swung open the door, and Stephen climbed the stairs behind him to the third-floor landing.

In the hallway, subdued lighting from brass wall sconces illuminated the long expanse from one end of the building to the other. A red exit sign glowed over a stairwell at the far end.

"Are these stairwells the only exits?" Stephen asked. "My wife worries about fire."

"Except for the elevators, yes, sir." Josiah stopped midway down the hall and used the room key to open a door located directly across from the elevators. "And the fire escape from this suite."

Stephen entered a room as tastefully decorated as the lobby. "Do all the rooms have fire escapes?"

"No, sir. The owner used to live here and had one installed when he had the balcony built." Josiah opened a pair of French doors and stepped onto a miniature balcony with a sweeping view of downtown Atlanta.

Stephen joined him on the balcony. "Quite a view."

"Yes, sir. And the fire escape leads down there." Josiah pointed to a one-story building that jutted out beyond the footprint of the main hotel. "That wing there is the restaurant. A fire escape at the south end of that building leads to the ground."

Stephen nodded. The suite was perfect with three avenues of escape, not counting the elevators. Satisfied, he returned to the lobby with Josiah via the elevator and motioned for Rachel to join him.

"The rooms are exactly what we need," Stephen

told the clerk as he signed the register and handed her a deposit from the cash Rachel had received for his check at a Flat Rock bank.

"We're happy to have you as our guests." The clerk swiveled the register toward her and glanced at Stephen's signature, "Dr. Newman, Mrs. Newman, let me assure you that our hotel has a state-of-the-art sprinkler and fire alarm system."

Rachel looked confused. "Thank you."

The clerk handed Stephen the room key. "If there's anything else you need—"

"As a matter of fact, there is," Stephen said. "Is it possible to get two weeks' back issues of the local paper?"

The clerk nodded. "I'm sure the concierge can accommodate you. Will tomorrow morning be soon enough?"

"Fine, thanks." Stephen grabbed the suitcase with one hand and Rachel's elbow with the other and steered her into the waiting elevator.

"Sprinkler system?" she asked with an amused look. "What was that all about?"

"I told the clerk you had a phobia of hotel fires."

"I thought we'd agreed not to call attention to ourselves."

"This was worth the risk. Not only do we have a room with a view, we have a balcony with a fire escape."

"Good work, Chandler. Your memory may be gone, but otherwise your brain is firing on all cylinders."

The bright approval shining in her face hit him like

a sucker punch. When the elevator doors slid open, he wanted nothing more than to lift her in his arms, carry her across the threshold, and—

Damn.

His brain couldn't be functioning all that well if he was allowing Rachel to distract him. Without his memory, he had to rely on his instincts, but how could he trust his sixth sense, when it was broadcasting patterns and undercurrents he didn't understand?

He opened the door to the suite and followed Rachel inside. She disappeared into the adjoining bedroom and immediately reemerged, her face flaming.

"What's going on?" she demanded.

"I've been wondering that myself."

"Don't tap-dance with me. There's only one bed in there."

He stepped to the bedroom doorway. A king-size bed with a quilted coverlet dominated one wall. Without warning, visions of Rachel, asleep in his arms, her blond hair spread across his bare chest, popped into his mind.

A fantasy?

The memory seemed too vivid, too real.

He turned back to Rachel, no longer the blonde of his dream but an auburn-haired spitfire who looked ready to chew nails. He'd never get the facts out of her if she didn't calm down first.

"No problem," he said. "I can sleep on one of the sofas in the sitting room."

"Sorry," she muttered, her anger changing quickly to embarrassment. "I shouldn't have jumped to conclusions. Nerves, I guess."

"It's more than nerves." He stepped close enough to place his hand beneath her chin and tilt her face until their gazes met. She tried to look away, but he held her fast. "You're not being straight with me. I can feel it."

She blinked rapidly, as if thinking quickly, shrugged off his hand and turned away. "You're imagining things."

"I thought so, too, at first. But the memory is too persistent. It has to be real."

She grew very still, almost as if she'd stopped breathing, and continued to stare out the window at the Atlanta skyline, avoiding his eyes. When she spoke, her voice was soft and tentative. "What memory?"

"You. Me. Together."

"Together?"

"Making love."

"That's...ridiculous."

"Is it? Then why do I feel like that's what I want more than anything else in the world this minute, to carry you into that bedroom and make love to you until we're both too weak to move?"

"Don't be silly." Her words were breathless, tinged with desperation. "We're like—"

"Brother and sister? I don't think so." In two quick strides, he reached her, twisted her toward him and wrapped his arms around her. He claimed her mouth with his, tasting her sweetness, and experienced the heady sensation of coming home after a long absence.

She resisted his embrace only for an instant before

yielding. Leaning against him, she stood on tiptoe to twine her fingers in his hair. He ran his hands from her shoulders to her waist, caressed her slender hips, then pushed aside her bulky sweater. When he touched the bare skin of her midriff, she gasped and jerked away.

"No," she cried. "We can't."

He drew in a lungful of air to steady himself. He had loved this woman. He'd stake his life on it.

"Look me in the eye," he said with a calm he didn't feel. "Swear to me we've never been together, and I promise not to touch you again."

She shook her head sadly. "It isn't that simple."

"The truth should be simple enough."

"But it isn't what it seems."

"Try me."

She took a deep breath and clasped her shaking hands in front of her. "We did make love, but only once. And that time was a mistake."

"Kissing you just now didn't feel like a mistake."

"Hormones," she said with a weak attempt at a smile. "You're in love with Anne Michelle, remember?"

"Forget Anne Michelle." The name had a familiar ring, but it evoked no emotion. "I'm talking about you and me. Tell me about the time we made love."

"It was after your going-away party. We'd both had too much to drink or it would never have happened."

He frowned. "That's it? I made love to you one time, then moved away?"

Her face reddened with her discomfort. She obviously didn't want to talk about their brief encounter. "I told you it was a mistake. Afterward we both knew it and decided to act as if it had never happened."

"What I experienced a few minutes ago didn't feel like a mistake. It felt right."

"Our lovemaking then was a mistake—"

"Because of Jessica's father?" he asked.

"Yes," she answered too quickly, "and it was a mistake just now because of Anne Michelle."

"Then you felt it, too?"

"That our kissing was wrong?"

"No. That it was perfect."

She raked her fingers through her hair in frustration. "How can you know it was perfect when you can't remember Anne Michelle?"

"If my feelings for this woman are so strong, why am I not remembering her instead of wanting to make love with you?"

"Because I'm here and she's not." Rachel straightened her sweater he had disarrayed and slung her purse over her shoulder. "We're talking in circles. I'm going for a walk."

"Alone?"

Her green eyes flashed. "I'm a big girl. I can take care of myself."

Before he could protest further, she was out the door and gone.

RACHEL WELCOMED the chill breeze against her heated cheeks, but wished she'd stopped long enough to grab a jacket. The sun had dipped lower in the sky, and the temperature was falling with it. Cooling off, however, was what she needed, so she didn't return to the hotel for a coat.

Instead, she headed toward downtown and the address listed on Anne Michelle's business card. She needed to imprint on her mind everything she could find about the woman Stephen loved, to remind herself of his commitment to someone else before she did something very foolish.

Cars and trucks clogged Peachtree Street, but pedestrian traffic was sparse as she hurried along the sidewalk. She glanced over her shoulder and realized she should be able to tell easily if someone was following her—on foot. But someone in a car could keep her under surveillance easily without her noticing in the rush hour congestion.

Less than twenty minutes later she approached the receptionist at the Creative Marketing offices on the eighth floor of the glass-clad skyscraper. "I'm looking for Anne Michelle Logan."

"Ms. Logan isn't taking any more appointments today," the pert young woman with bouffant blond hair announced.

"She's here?" Rachel asked in surprise, wondering if Stephen had failed to warn Anne Michelle after all.

"Yes, but she's not seeing anyone else today," the receptionist reiterated. "Would you like an appointment for tomorrow? I have a ten o'clock opening."

Rachel thought fast. If she could talk with Anne Michelle without revealing Stephen's whereabouts, the woman might have knowledge of who was after them. And, Rachel admitted, Anne Michelle should be warned that she, too, could be in danger. Tomorrow morning might be too late.

"I think Ms. Logan will see me," Rachel said. "Tell her I'd like to speak with her regarding Stephen Chandler."

The young woman look flustered. "Stephen Chandler?"

"She'll know the name."

The receptionist frowned. "Without a doubt, but—"

"I don't have time to play games. Tell Ms. Logan it's a matter of life and death."

The young woman looked as if she was going to refuse before she relented with a sigh. "Your name?"

"Harriet Bond," Rachel said, reluctant to reveal her identity in case her pursuers contacted Anne Michelle's office. "I'm with the FBI."

With obvious reluctance the receptionist rose from her desk, scurried down a hallway to the right and disappeared into an office. Within seconds she returned. "Ms. Logan will see you now."

Rachel followed the receptionist's earlier path down the hall and entered a spacious office with floor-to-ceiling windows that offered a spectacular view of Stone Mountain in the distance. Behind a French provincial desk of bleached oak sat a woman in her early thirties, her blond hair swept into an elegant twist, her green eyes a few shades lighter than the Chanel suit that showed off her perfect figure.

She stood when Rachel entered. "Have a seat, Ms. Bond. What can I do for you?"

"I'm here about Stephen Chandler."

"That's what Peggy said. How is Stephen?" Anne Michelle's voice was polite, but cool.

"He's disappeared."

"He does that often when he's working on a case. Part of the job, he always told me."

"When was the last time you saw him?"

Anne Michelle gave an ironic laugh and jammed her hands into the pockets of her expensive jacket. "I don't think I can be much help. I haven't seen Stephen since last May."

"Last May?" Surprise robbed Rachel of breath, and she sank into an upholstered Empire chair in front of the desk. "But aren't you and Stephen married?"

"We were only engaged," Anne Michelle said with a frown. "For an FBI agent, your intelligence isn't very up-to-date. Stephen broke our engagement six months ago."

"*Stephen* broke the engagement?"

Anne Michelle shrugged. "It happens."

"I'm sorry. I...didn't know."

"Obviously. Am I a suspect in his disappearance?"

Rachel shook her head. "I, uh, that is, the Bureau thought Stephen might have contacted you, told you where he was going and why."

The attractive blonde settled into her desk chair, picked up a sterling silver letter opener with a filigree handle and twirled it between her fingers. "As far as I'm concerned, Stephen disappeared a long time ago. We haven't been in contact since our breakup."

Rachel's mind boggled at the fact that Stephen apparently *didn't* love Anne Michelle, and she was having trouble thinking straight.

"I'm sorry," Rachel repeated.

"Don't be," the woman said with a warm smile. "It was for the best. One of the things that attracted me to Stephen in the first place was his honesty. He was straightforward enough to admit it when he realized he'd been attracted to me because I reminded him of someone else."

Rachel's bubble of happiness burst. "You reminded him of someone else?"

Anne Michelle nodded. "A green-eyed blonde he called Doc. Know her?"

"I don't think so."

Doc? Stephen loved *her?*

Was that why he'd tried so often to call her after his going-away party and for weeks after his move to Atlanta? He'd been in love with her, and she'd been so afraid of being hurt again she'd refused to recognize his feelings for what they really were.

Rachel shoved to her feet, anxious to escape Anne Michelle's office and order her whirling thoughts. "I'd better be going."

Anne Michelle's gaze took on a faraway look, as if she'd forgotten Rachel was in the room. "Stephen said as much as he hated calling off the wedding, he'd be an even worse cad if he married me under false pretenses. Stephen Chandler is one of the most honorable men I've every met. Just my luck things didn't work out between us."

"I'm sorry," Rachel murmured.

"Did he marry his Doc?"

"No," Rachel said with a catch in her voice.

"Too bad. From the way he talked about her, she

was the love of his life. I'd have never had a chance with him in the first place if he hadn't been on the rebound.''

The woman had to be mistaken. Stephen hadn't loved Rachel. Or had he? Had she been too blinded by her fear of being hurt to see it? Her heart constricted with the pain of opportunities missed, time wasted. Not only had she sacrificed her chance for happiness, but she'd cheated both Stephen and Jessica.

Her vision blurring with unshed tears, Rachel headed toward the door. ''Thank you for your time.''

Anne Michelle rose and walked with her into the hallway. ''Is Stephen in danger?''

Rachel read the concern in the woman's eyes and wondered if she was still in love with her ex-fiancé. ''Stephen is a trained agent. He can take care of himself.''

Anne Michelle's expression was bittersweet. ''When you find him…''

''Yes?''

''Give him my regards.''

Rachel hurried from the office. When she reached the street, the sun was setting, shadows from the tall buildings had deepened, and the temperature had dropped. But the cold was the least of her problems.

Anne Michelle's revelations made her head spin. Stephen *loved* her? During the four years they'd worked as partners, she had closed herself off to that prospect, refusing to risk her emotions after Brad had trounced them—and her self-esteem—so thoroughly. After Brad's deception, she hadn't conceded the possibility that a man like Stephen Chandler could love her. And she certainly hadn't been willing to risk loving again, no matter how wonderful Stephen had been.

But she'd only been fooling herself. She had loved Stephen all along. And she loved him now.

But now was too late.

Stephen would hate her when he discovered she'd had his child and hidden Jessica from him. Her own deception was as cruel as Brad's had been and destroyed any chances of a life with Stephen. As Anne Michelle had stressed, he was an honorable man, and he would find Rachel's betrayal reprehensible.

Unforgivable.

She trudged back toward the hotel, her heart as cold as the night air.

STEPHEN TRIED to stretch his legs and banged his feet against the too-short sofa. He might as well get up. He hadn't slept all night. And from the sounds of tossing and turning that had emanated all hours from the adjacent bedroom and the current splash of the shower, Rachel hadn't slept, either.

She'd returned from her downtown trek looking as if her world was coming to an end and refusing to talk about whatever was bothering her. Fragments of images tickled his mind. If he could only remember, maybe he could figure out what Rachel was hiding from him.

He was certain she was hiding something. There had to have been more than an inebriated one-night stand between them. The feelings he had for her hadn't developed out of thin air. She must be lying. Why else wouldn't she look him in the eye?

He kicked off the tangled blanket, rose, and was pulling on his jeans when a knock sounded at the door. He grabbed his gun from the table. "Who is it?"

"The concierge, Dr. Newman. I have your back issues of the *Constitution*."

Stephen tucked the gun in the waist of his jeans at the small of his back and opened the door. The concierge entered and placed a stack of newspapers on the coffee table. Stephen slipped him a five, and the man left.

"Who was that?" Rachel stood in the bedroom doorway, dressed in hunter-green tights and matching pullover, her cheeks pink from her shower, her gaze avoiding his.

"The concierge brought the newspapers."

"Good," she said, too brightly. "I'll order breakfast from room service and help you read through them."

Stephen went into the bathroom to shower and dress. When he returned, a rolling table with their breakfast stood before the French doors opening onto the balcony. Rachel had opened the draperies to a gray, drizzly day.

He sat in a chair across the table from her and poured himself a cup of coffee. Rachel grasped her cup in both hands and stared out the window, her expression as bleak as the dreary morning.

"You okay?" he asked.

She nodded without conviction. "I just didn't sleep well. Must have been the strange bed."

He knew the feeling, but he also knew there was more to her unhappiness than a poor night's rest. "Something's bothering you."

"I'm separated from my daughter and on the run for my life," she said hotly. "Why should anything be bothering me?"

He held up his hands in surrender. "Sorry. I don't mean to pry. I was just hoping to help with whatever it is."

"You can't." Her magnificent green eyes welled with sadness, "But thanks for asking."

"You're not eating."

"I'm not hungry."

He wanted to encourage her to eat, but sensed she'd resent his prodding. His memories of her had been returning in a flurry of snapshot images, Rachel riding beside him in the car on the way to a stakeout, smiling across a table in a Savannah restaurant, handcuffing a suspect, comforting the family of a shooting victim. Along with the recollections came emotions, powerful and strong.

How could he be married or even engaged to someone else when he loved Rachel with an intensity that shook him to his bones? And why could he recall that he loved her, but not the identities of the people who stalked them?

He reached across the table and grasped her hand. "Where did you go yesterday when you left the hotel?"

She sighed and raised her gaze to his. The sadness

in her eyes startled him. "You have a right to know," she said with obvious reluctance.

Steeling himself for what was apparently going to be bad news, he nodded for her to continue.

"I went to Anne Michelle's office."

"You could have been spotted," he said angrily.

"But I wasn't. I doubt anyone was watching your ex-fiancée, anyway."

"How could you be sure—" her words finally sank in. "*Ex*-fiancée?"

Rachel pulled her hand from his and stared at her coffee cup. "She hasn't seen you or spoken with you in over six months."

"She was there? You saw her?"

"She sends her regards."

He attempted to clear his jumbled thoughts. He'd been engaged, then unengaged, but he had no memory of Anne Michelle Logan. "What does she look like?"

Rachel squirmed in her chair. "She's beautiful. Blond hair, green eyes."

"Like you."

"Not like me," Rachel protested. "Anne Michelle is drop-dead gorgeous. And she's several inches taller than I am."

No memories of Anne Michelle came to his aid. Not a glimmer of emotion except puzzlement and an overwhelming relief. His feelings for Doc betrayed no one. He was free to pursue those feelings, if she would accept them. She'd consented to his kiss, but he wanted them to share more.

Rachel glanced at her watch. "I have to call the

Kidbroughs. Mom said she would be at their house this morning so I can talk to her, too.''

She had disappeared into the bedroom to use the phone before Stephen realized he hadn't asked why his engagement to Anne Michelle had ended. The suspicion that Rachel knew more than she was saying nagged at him.

She was smiling when she reentered the room. ''Jessica was giggling the whole time I was talking with Mom. It's good to know she's happy.''

Unwilling to ruin Rachel's pleasant mood, he suppressed his lingering questions about Anne Michelle and nodded toward the stack of newspapers of the coffee table. ''We have our work cut out for us. What do you think? Should we start with two weeks ago and work forward?''

She shook her head. ''Let's start with today and work backward.''

He handed her the current issue, deliberately touching her, letting his hand skim her delicate wrist. She scanned the front page quickly, then flipped it open, hiding herself from his scrutiny behind the pages. He sat beside her, draped his arm around her shoulders and began to read the previous day's paper. Slowly, almost imperceptibly, she drew away.

With a sigh he accepted her withdrawal and concentrated on his reading. He had almost finished the local news section when his glance fell on a small headline: Killer of White Supremacist Still at Large. His own name jumped out at him from the article that followed.

"This is it," he said to Rachel. "I've found something."

"What?" She lowered her paper and leaned toward him. The scent of her shampoo filled his nostrils, making him momentarily forget his train of thought.

He found his place again on the page and began reading aloud. "'Atlanta police and the FBI have no leads in the assassination of a white supremacist who was shot in Atlanta last week—'"

A knock at the door interrupted him.

"Who is it?" he called.

"Room service," came the reply.

He glanced at Rachel. "Did you order anything else?"

"No."

His instincts screamed danger. "You must have the wrong room," he called.

"This *is* 345," the voice insisted.

"Quick," he whispered to Rachel, "out the balcony and down the fire escape. I'll be right behind you."

She sprang from the table, grabbed her purse and darted to the French doors.

"Hurry!" His heart raced with fear for her.

In an instant she had disappeared over the edge of the balcony and started down the ladder.

Before he could follow, a crash reverberated inside the suite as the door banged open. Stephen plunged through the open French doors and swung his leg over the balcony rail.

"Hold it right there or I'll shoot," a harsh voice ordered.

Stephen turned slowly, hands raised.

An angry-looking man in a brown leather jacket pointed a Glock pistol at him. "Where's Rachel Goforth?"

Stephen shrugged.

Keeping his weapon trained on Stephen, the intruder did a quick search of the suite, then turned his attention on Stephen, considering him with a puzzled expression. "You have a lot of questions to answer, Chandler."

Questions?

Stephen had a few of his own. Like why the man hadn't shot him already. Stephen nodded toward the pistol pointed at him. "That's a very persuasive interrogator."

"Get back inside," the man said. "Keep your hands where I can see them and don't make any quick moves."

Stephen flicked a glance below and spotted Rachel, sprinting across the restaurant roof toward the metal ladder that led to the ground.

He breathed a sigh of relief. The intruder was probably going to kill him, but Rachel, at least, had escaped.

Chapter Ten

Believing Stephen was right behind her, Rachel dashed across the roof of the restaurant kitchen to the fire escape at the far end of the building. Turning to descend the ladder, she glanced back at the balcony and caught a glimpse of Stephen, reentering the hotel room, hands raised.

She stopped, torn by the desire to rush back to help him.

If he'd been captured by members of the hate group he'd been reading about in the newspaper before the knock on the door, he was in terrible danger. A new recruit, eager to earn the right to wear the infamous spiderweb tattoo, would snuff out Stephen's life in the blink of an eye.

She couldn't leave the man she loved, the father of her child. Just thinking about the danger he faced froze her in indecision. She had to help him.

Stepping back onto the roof, she hesitated, then discarded the direct line of approach. The intruder would be less likely to spot her if she circled and reentered the building and advanced from the hallway. She could ambush them leaving the suite.

Unless they plan to kill Stephen in the hotel room.

Shoving the unbearable thought away, she returned to the ladder and scampered down, her bulky shoulder bag banging against her hip. Her feet hit the ground, and she turned, primed to run toward the hotel entrance.

A tall man stood waiting only a few feet away. With thick, gray hair, silver-framed glasses and a rumpled blue suit, he had a benign, grandfatherly appearance.

Except for the gun trained on her.

"Stop where you are," he ordered. "Hands in the air. You've led us on a hell of a chase."

She tried to brazen her way out. "What do you want with me?"

"You'll know soon enough." He approached cautiously and snatched the bag from her shoulder.

Gone was any hope of reaching for her gun. Her heart thrashed against her breastbone in panic, and she bit her lower lip to keep from screaming.

She had to reach Stephen.

Without realizing it, she must have spoken his name aloud.

"Don't worry about Stephen," her captor said. "My partner's taking care of him."

Fear shuddered through her. "That's what I'm afraid of."

"We're going back into the hotel." He waved her on with his gun. "You walk ahead. And don't make any sudden moves. I'm right behind you."

Her hopes resurged. She could cause a diversion in the lobby that would draw attention—and help.

Her captor must have read her mind. "Don't try anything funny. We'll go in the back entrance and up the service elevator. We've cleared the hallways, so there're no witnesses around."

"Who are you?" she asked over her shoulder. "What do you want with me?"

Ignoring her query, he pushed her ahead of him toward a steel door at the rear of the restaurant. "I'll ask the questions."

She refused to return inside with her captor. If she couldn't rescue Stephen, she had to run, to save herself for Jessica's sake. She silently vowed that her daughter wouldn't grow up an orphan.

Abruptly she wheeled, shoulder down, and caught her captor by surprise. He let out an "umph" as she knocked away his gun, hit him in the midriff, forcing the air from his lungs. His weapon hit the pavement. As he scrambled for his pistol, she ran. Racing as fast as her Doc Martens would carry her, she sprinted down Peachtree Street, away from the hotel.

Footsteps hammered the pavement behind her, and any moment she expected the sharp report of gunfire and a bullet in her back.

"Stop, damn it!"

The yell sounded too close, and she poured on speed.

But not enough.

Her captor caught her in a flying tackle. Windmilling her arms in an effort to remain upright, she tumbled to the sidewalk and cracked her face against the concrete.

The world went black.

RELIEVED THAT RACHEL had managed to flee down the fire escape, Stephen stepped off the balcony into the room. The man in the leather jacket had closed the door to the hallway and stood with his back against it, his gun trained on Stephen. His carrot-red hair, startling blue eyes and cocky grin seemed familiar.

"Who are you?" Stephen demanded. "What do you want?"

The man blinked in astonishment. "You don't know me?"

"Should I?"

"Are you kidding?" He looked surprised. "A man in your custody was murdered and you disappeared, without a word to anyone. It's been hell tracking you down, figuring out what you're up to. Like I said, you have a ton of questions to answer."

Stephen's confusion grew. The man didn't talk like an assassin, but Stephen refused to lower his guard.

Not yet.

The intruder scanned the room and spotted Stephen's pistol on an end table. Keeping his weapon aimed at Stephen, he crossed the room quickly, grabbed the Glock, and shoved it into his belt.

"Sit down—" he motioned Stephen toward the couch "—and keep your hands where I can see them."

Stephen sank onto the sofa and placed his hands

on his knees. His mind whirred, clicking through his options for escape, discarding them all as implausible, then grasping the most risky as his only chance. He'd try to catch the gunman by surprise and overpower him.

"You really don't know me?" The man's expression was incredulous.

"You're probably my worst nightmare. Sorry if I can't remember. I've had amnesia since a knock on the head a few days ago." Stephen measured the distance from the sofa to his captor. When he leaped, the man would probably shoot him, but if he twisted to the right—

The gunman smiled with genuine warmth, settled into the chair across from Stephen and lowered his weapon. "That explains a hell of a lot."

"Like what?" His captor's sudden friendly demeanor surprised Stephen and ruined his chance to spring. He'd have to wait for a better opportunity to break for the door. And hope he had one. If he was lucky, the man wouldn't kill him before Rachel returned with help.

The intruder reached into his leather jacket, extracted a thin leather folder, and tossed it to Stephen. Stephen flipped it open. Inside were the photo ID and golden eagle badge of FBI agent Jack Roche.

Warring instincts buffeted him. The name Jack Roche didn't raise any red flags in his sparse recollections, but Stephen was still wary. "You're FBI?"

"More than FBI, my friend. I've been your partner for over a year."

"Then why are you holding a gun on me?"

"We've been looking for you for days. Ever since you disappeared when Milton Carver was killed."

"You think *I* killed him?"

Jack shrugged. "Stranger things have happened. Why else would you disappear? When we finally located you at the motel in Flat Rock with Rachel Goforth, we couldn't figure out what was going on. We didn't know if she was in cahoots with you in Carver's murder or was holding you against your will."

"Neither," Stephen said.

Jack studied him and shook his head. "You *really* don't remember me?"

A memory resurfaced and clicked into place. "Better than a sharp stick in the eye?"

"Huh?"

"Isn't that one of your favorite expressions?"

"You *do* remember."

Stephen shook his head in frustration. "Not enough. That single arcane fragment is the sum total of my recollections of you."

"Why did you run after Carver died?"

"It's a long story," Stephen said, still uncertain how much to trust Jack, even though instinct assured him his partner was a friend.

In the hallway knuckles rapped sharply on the door.

"Who is it?" Jack called.

"Pete."

Jack holstered his weapon and opened the door.

Stephen leaped to his feet at the sight of Rachel, blood trickling from a cut on her cheekbone. Oblivious of her captor holding a gun, he rushed to her, gathered her in his arms and held her close. "What happened?"

She pulled away and jerked her thumb over her shoulder toward the man named Pete. "I almost escaped, but he tackled me."

Anger rising to a boil, Stephen turned on Pete. "That's a hell of a way to treat a woman."

Pete shrugged and looked sheepish. "For all we knew, she'd been holding you hostage. I couldn't let her get away without questioning her."

Stephen returned his attention to Rachel, inspecting her at arm's length. "You didn't break any bones?"

She shook her head. "A few bruises, maybe. What's going on?"

Happy to have her close, yet still wishing she'd managed to escape, he flashed her a rueful smile. "We've been captured by the Bureau."

Her expression turned to puzzlement. "What are you talking about?"

Stephen nodded toward the Pete and Jack. "They're FBI."

Rachel studied their captors with narrowed eyes before returning her gaze to his. "You're sure?"

"I'm Jack Roche." Jack handed her his ID folder. "My partner is Pete Elkins."

Rachel scrutinized the card and badge. "Your credentials are legit, but why is the FBI after us?"

"I'll explain everything later," Jack said, "but first, I'm taking you both to a doctor."

Rachel swiped at her bleeding cheek with the back of her hand. "For a simple cut? Forget it. I'm not going anywhere until you tell me what's going on."

"It's not just the cut on your pretty face that concerns me," Jack said.

"It's me, isn't it?" Stephen asked. "You want to make sure my amnesia's not an act."

"We'll have you both checked out," Jack said. "Then you'll answer our questions."

"We've got killers on our heels," Stephen said. "Can you guarantee our safety?"

Jack shot him a strange look. "Like you guaranteed Milton Carver's?"

Stephen didn't answer. According to the newspaper article he'd been reading when Jack arrived, Milton Carver was the white supremacist who'd been shot while in FBI custody. Stephen's custody.

Jack Roche wanted answers.

And Stephen didn't have them.

RACHEL RUBBED HER EYES with her fists, stretched her arms to relieve the tension in her back and checked her watch. Six o'clock in the evening.

They had spent the morning at the hospital, where an emergency room doctor had stitched the cut in her cheek and given her a tetanus booster. Then she'd waited with Pete and Jack while a neurologist ran an MRI on Stephen and verified his loss of memory.

Satisfied with Stephen's truthfulness, the agents had driven her and Stephen back to FBI headquarters and placed them in separate interrogation rooms. For the entire afternoon Pete had grilled her with questions about the past few days, while Jack subjected Stephen to the same procedure. Pete had left the room an hour ago. Relying on her knowledge of FBI protocol, she guessed that Jack and Pete were comparing notes on what they'd learned, while Stephen, like her, cooled his heels in another room.

The door opened, and Pete stuck his head in. "Come with me."

She slung the strap of her purse over her shoulder and followed the agent down the hall to a small lobby where Stephen and Jack waited. Her heart stuttered at Stephen's welcoming smile, and she avoided his gaze to keep from giving her own feelings away.

"Am I under arrest?" she asked.

Jack shook his head and returned their weapons. "You've answered all our questions and your stories check out."

"I have questions of my own," Stephen said.

"And we owe you answers," Jack said. "After what we've put you through today, I'd say we also owe you dinner."

Rachel and Stephen accompanied Jack and Pete to an Italian restaurant around the corner of the Federal Building where the FBI offices were located. The agents were obviously well-known at the eatery. The hostess greeted them by name, including Stephen, and led them to a secluded booth at the rear of the dining room where they could speak freely without being overheard.

Rachel still felt like a prisoner, however, when Jack motioned Stephen to one side of the booth, her to the other, and he and Pete sat on the ends as if blocking their escape.

As soon as they'd placed their orders, Stephen

turned to Jack. "How about those answers you promised me?"

Jack's intense blue eyes shone in the glimmer of the candle that dripped wax on its Chianti-bottle holder in the center of the table. "Five days ago, you and I were transporting Milton Carver back to lockup after questioning."

"We made the collar?" Stephen asked.

Jack nodded. "We'd spent months working the case. Thanks to an informant's tip, Carver was our chief suspect in a chain of arsons against several African-American churches in the Atlanta area."

"Did he confess?" Rachel asked.

"According to the transcript of the interrogation," Jack said, "Carver didn't give up anything. But you—" he nodded to Stephen "—sat in the back seat and talked to him all the way across town. I was driving and didn't hear most of the conversation, so I don't know if he confessed anything during the ride."

"With Carver dead," Pete added, "we'll never know. Unless you get your memory back."

"How did he die?" Stephen asked.

"We were stopped at a light," Jack said. "An armor-piercing bullet came through the rear window and struck Carver in the back of the head. He died instantly."

"I was sitting next to him," Stephen said. "Are you sure he was the target?"

Jack took a sip of water and shrugged. "Can't be certain until we catch the gunman. That's what you were intending to do the last time I saw you."

Stephen's dark eyes lit with excitement, reminding

Rachel of their daughter's. "I remember. I saw a glint of metal, like a rifle barrel, in an open, third-floor window."

Pete leaned forward. "Anything else?"

Stephen's shoulders drooped, and he shook his head in disappointment. "Just that one flash."

"It's like the neurologist said," Rachel assured him, proud of his composure under such pressure. "You may recall lots of bits and pieces before your memory returns in full."

"*If* it returns in full," Stephen reminded her. He turned to Jack. "What happened after Carver was shot?"

"You took off down the street in search of the gunman while I waited for forensics and the coroner."

"And that's the last you saw or heard from me until today?"

Jack nodded.

"How did you find him?" Rachel asked.

"When Stephen didn't check in and we were unable to locate him," Pete said, "the Bureau put out an APB."

She suddenly understood. "Including his bank account and credit card numbers in case anyone had harmed Stephen and stolen them."

"Right." Jack flashed her an approving grin. "Stephen always said you were sharp, Doc."

Wondering how much Stephen had talked about her to his current partner, Rachel flushed and hoped the dim lighting of the restaurant hid her embarrassment. "So how did you pick up our trail from North Carolina?"

"When the Hendersonville bank notified us it had cashed one of Stephen's checks," Jack said, "we moved in. They had video of you, your car and license number from their security cameras. It didn't take long to track you down through the rental car agency and spot your rented Blazer at the motel where you were staying."

Stephen frowned. "If you located us that night, why did you wait two days to make contact?"

"To be honest," Jack said, "we couldn't figure out what the hell was going on. Since you hadn't alerted the Bureau concerning the reason for your disappearance, we couldn't discount the possibility that you were up to something illegal."

"Your disguises," Pete added, "didn't exactly alleviate our suspicions."

"We decided to follow you," Jack said, "to see if we could figure out what you were up to. After two days we still didn't have a clue. Figured the only way to find out was to detain you and ask."

"Are you satisfied?" Rachel demanded, wondering if the agents really were going to release them.

"That you're clean?" Jack asked. "Yeah, but I'm not satisfied with so many unanswered questions."

"Like who killed Carver," Stephen said, reminding Rachel that one of the things she loved most about him was his unswerving determination to close a case.

Jack nodded. "And who's after you and your former partner."

"And why," Pete added.

"Guess I'll have to return to work and find out," Stephen said. "Can Rachel use a safe house in the meantime?"

Jack and Pete exchanged uneasy glances before Jack spoke. "You're on medical leave, Chandler. According to the doctor's report, you can't return to work until you have your memory back. Too dangerous for you, otherwise."

"We can put you both in a safe house," Pete said, "and provide round-the-clock protection until we arrest who's after you."

Rachel glanced across the table at Stephen. A frown created hatch marks between his eyebrows, and his dark eyes clouded. She'd seen that look many times before. She knew him so well. Knew when he was happy, angry or sad. This time she recognized that Stephen's intuition had kicked in.

"We're free to go?" he asked.

"You haven't broken any laws," Jack said, "but—"

"I can't sit and hide," Stephen said. "I'd like to follow a few leads of my own."

"Unofficially, of course," Rachel added hastily, afraid Jack and Pete would order Stephen and her not to interfere.

"What kind of leads?" Jack asked.

"The Atlanta office is concentrating on solving Carver's murder, right?" Stephen said.

Pete nodded. "Right."

"Then Rachel and I will go to Savannah."

"Why Savannah?" Jack asked.

"According to Rachel, before I lost my memory, I

told her whoever's after us is connected to a case we worked together there. I'm hoping that's where we'll find answers.''

Jack scowled. ''You could also find a killer waiting for you.''

Stephen's expression settled into hard, resolute lines. ''Whoever's after us is determined. Our going into hiding won't make him go away. Our best bet is to draw him out. Make him show himself.''

''The 'he' you're referring to,'' Jack said gravely, ''could be an entire army of white supremacists, out for revenge.''

''All the more reason to find them and let the authorities deal with them,'' Rachel said. ''We can't allow a group of extremists to take the law into their own hands.''

''Spoken like a true agent,'' Pete said with an approving grin. ''With commitment like that, what made you leave the Bureau, Ms. Goforth?''

The waitress's arrival to take their order saved Rachel from answering. Hiding behind her menu, she could feel Stephen's curious gaze and wondered if he'd remembered anything else about their relationship. Her heart hammered with fear at the possibility he might calculate Jessica's age and draw his own conclusions about her paternity before Rachel had the right opportunity to tell him the truth. Certainly the right time wasn't now, flanked by two curious agents. She prayed she'd get through this dinner.

At eight o'clock Jack drove Rachel and Stephen back to their hotel, where they would spend the night before heading to Savannah in the morning. While

Stephen finished reading newspaper accounts of the arrest and death of Milton Carver, Rachel telephoned the Kidbroughs, who assured her that her parents and Jessica were fine. Next she placed a call to her boss and extended her personal leave for several more days.

She knew now was the time to confess to Stephen about Jessica, but she ached too much with tension and fatigue. She could hardly stay awake, much less talk straight. She needed to be fresh and alert when she broached that touchy subject.

She slipped into the massive, marble-tiled bathroom of the suite, filled the oversize whirlpool tub with steaming water and complementary bubble bath and removed her clothes. The hotel had provided all the amenities, even groupings of scented, columnar candles on the vanity and at the tub's edge. She lit them and turned off the overhead light. With a grateful sigh, she slid into hot water up to her chin and rested her head against the tub's edge.

The pulsing water eased the tension in her muscles, but it couldn't calm her thoughts. How had she managed to make such a mess of her life? Bad enough that she hadn't recognized and accepted her love for Stephen when they were working together, but now— how was she going to tell him that Jessica was his daughter? That knowledge was no longer a threat to him, now that she knew he wasn't in love with Anne Michelle. He had a right to know.

And a right to be mad as hell that she hadn't told him before.

But she shouldn't hit him with that bombshell

while they were searching for killers on their trail, she rationalized. He shouldn't be distracted. He had enough on his plate dealing with lost memories and hidden assassins. She'd tell him, she promised herself, as soon as the white supremacists were caught.

That decision took care of one problem. But how was she to deal with the other, the fact that she loved Stephen so desperately he could probably read it all over her face? He'd loved her once. She realized that now. But he wouldn't love her after he learned of her deception. She had to keep her feelings to herself and be ready to walk away once she'd told him the truth about Jessica.

He'd want parental custody, of course, and she might have to see him every other weekend for the next eighteen years. The prospect of seeing Stephen that often without having his love brought tears to her eyes.

"You okay, Doc?"

As if her thoughts had conjured him up, Stephen stood in the bathroom doorway, his muscular body silhouetted by lights in the room behind him. She couldn't discern his expression in the shadows.

"I'm fine," she answered, silently cursing the break in her voice. She wiped away the tears, leaving a trail of bubbles on her cheeks.

"You're missing Jessica, aren't you?"

"Yes." That was only part of her sadness. She couldn't tell him the rest.

Swiftly and silently, he crossed the room and knelt on the thick rug beside the tub. The magnificent planes of his face glowed in the candlelight, and his dark eyes gleamed with a warmth she couldn't face.

"I'm sorry," he said.

"For what?"

"For dragging you into this mess."

"Your alert probably saved my life. And Jessica's."

Gently he wiped the bubbles from her cheeks. "But you don't deserve this—being separated from your baby, shot at, interrogated."

"Fortunately—" she forced a smile "—most of us never get what we truly deserve."

He cupped her face in his palm, turning her gaze to his. "I remember, Doc."

She sucked in a startled breath, and her pulse pounded in alarm. "Remember?"

He nodded and leaned closer until she was drowning in the warm, mahogany depths of his eyes. "I remember that I love you."

"No," she breathed, her defenses weakening.

"It's true. I tried to forget you when I left Savannah, but I couldn't. When I met Anne Michelle, I didn't realize the attraction was her resemblance to you."

She caught her lower lip in her teeth to keep from groaning. He *had* remembered. Coward that she was, she hadn't told him what Anne Michelle had said. She was a coward, all right, or she would have told him then about his daughter.

Their daughter.

"Know what my instincts tell me?" he asked. His lips were so close she could feel the titillating warmth of his breath against her mouth. She wanted him, but didn't deserve him, didn't deserve to feel anything but his anger.

She shook her head, afraid to trust her voice.

"My instincts tell me you love me, too."

She swallowed against the lump in her throat. "Your instincts are wrong."

"Uh-uh." He ran his fingers through her hair, caressed her earlobe, traced a gentle circle around the stitches on her cheek. "They're never wrong."

She tried to look away from the passion burning in his eyes, but he held her fast. "You remember that?"

He shook his head. "You told me, just a few days ago."

"Then *I* was wrong."

Sliding his arms around her, he pressed his lips to hers. Unable to resist the closeness, she raised her arms around his neck and opened her lips. She needed him one last time, before he learned what she'd done, the lies she'd told him, the daughter she'd robbed him of.

His kiss, at first gentle and seeking, intensified, crashing her remaining barriers, destroying her defenses, squelching the inner voice that warned her to break away, but she couldn't fight the magnitude of her own desire.

Couldn't speak.

Couldn't breathe...

Stephen drew back and threw her a challenging glance. "Tell me now you don't love me."

She opened her mouth, but the words wouldn't come.

"That's what I thought," he said with a self-satisfied chuckle.

Happiness shot through her at his smile, but she couldn't revel in it. She had to end this before she yielded further. In desperation, she changed the subject. "Your shirt. It's soaked."

"Then I'd better take it off." He locked his gaze with hers as he undid one button after the other, then shrugged free of the wet garment. His muscles gleamed in the candlelight, taking her breath away.

"No point in getting the rest of my clothes wet." He unbuckled his belt, shucked slacks, shorts and shoes, and stood beside the tub, looking more awesome than her treasured memories of the one night she'd spent with him.

She had to stop him. Had to stop herself. He thought he loved her now, but when he learned about Jessica, he'd regret that he'd kissed her again.

"You'll get cold," she warned, goose bumps rising in spite of the hot water surrounding her.

"I have no intention of getting cold," he said with a cavalier grin. "You're going to keep me warm..."

Before she could protest, he stepped into the tub, sat beside her, and tugged her into his arms.

"...by showing me how much you love me."

End this now. Get out of the tub, her inner voice warned. *You'll only break your heart....*

"Shut up," she commanded her conscience.

"What?" he murmured in her ear.

"Kiss me." She didn't have to ask twice.

Claiming her mouth with his, he slid along the

length of her, their bodies gliding against each other beneath the water with the friction of silk on silk.

She cleared her thoughts of everything except the firmness of his back muscles beneath her hands, the familiar, virile scent that filled her nostrils, the honeyed taste of his mouth on hers. Her senses leaped in response. She arched beneath him, opening herself to him with a moan of delight. This was where she wanted to be, in his arms, in his life.

With frenzied tenderness, his passion intensified, drawing her with him in a whirlwind of excitement until an explosion of sensation left them breathless.

He turned onto his back and drew her against him with her head resting on his chest, just above the water.

"I love you, Doc."

A sob caught in her throat. He loved her now. She believed him without a doubt. But when she told him about Jessica...

Seizing this happiness to cherish and remember, she would worry about the consequences later.

She snuggled deeper into his embrace. "I've always loved you."

Chapter Eleven

Whistling lightly beneath his breath, Stephen lowered the Blazer's visor against the glare of the morning sun. His fingers tapped a happy rhythm on the steering wheel.

In the passenger seat Rachel stretched and yawned. "For a man who's had very little sleep, you're amazingly cheerful."

Her warm teasing bolstered his contentment. "Why shouldn't I be?"

"Just a few minor details, like a killer on our trail and your loss of memory."

"I remember very clearly every detail of last night." He shot her a suggestive smile and was rewarded by the brilliant pink that suffused her cheeks.

She wriggled uneasily against her seat belt. "Last night shouldn't have happened."

His cheerfulness faded. "Regrets?"

"It's more complicated than that."

"What's complicated about loving each other?" he insisted. Desire stirred again as he recalled how he'd lifted her from the tub, wrapped her in a gigantic towel and carried her to the king-size bed. Their love-making had lasted until the early morning, when, exhausted, they'd fallen asleep in each other's arms.

And awakened the same way.

That simple act, which reverberated with a memory he couldn't fully capture, convinced him he wanted to wake up every day with Rachel beside him. She had seemed happy enough this morning when she first opened her eyes. Obviously she was having second thoughts.

"There's too much you don't remember." Her pensive expression cast a cloud on the bright morning. "Your feelings will change when your memories return."

"Not a chance," he uttered with unshakable conviction. "What about your feelings? You admitted last night you love me—"

"I do."

He reached across the console that divided the seats, grasped her hand and raised her palm to his lips. "That's all that matters."

"If only…"

"If only what?"

"No point in agonizing over might-have-beens." She forced a weak smile. "Personal feelings will have to wait. We have a case to solve. Just like old times."

He ached to identify the source of her sadness and obliterate it, since nothing pleased him more than her happiness, but between his scant memories and his close observation of Rachel the past few days, he realized she couldn't be forced to reveal her secrets. He would have to wait until she was ready to share them.

Steering onto the ramp of the interstate that would take them to Savannah, he yielded to her change of subject. "Any ideas how to tackle our Savannah search?"

"We should go first to the FBI office and leave a message for Jason Bender."

He frowned. "That name makes me uneasy."

"Why?"

"The man just happens to be on vacation while you and I are being stalked? Too much of a coincidence."

"You're way off base," Rachel said. "In all the years I've known him, Jason has gone hiking every fall."

"But there's something—"

"Your instincts?"

He shook his head. "For some strange reason, everything about him is a void. Not only do I have no memories of him, but no gut feelings to fall back, on either."

"You needn't worry about Jason. He was one of your best friends."

"Was?"

"During the time you worked together in Savannah. Once I moved away, I don't know how long you kept in touch after your transfer to Atlanta. It was Jason—"

"Yes?"

Her appealing blush returned. "Jason told me about you and Anne Michelle."

Stephen grimaced. "But he didn't bother to tell you when the engagement ended."

"I—I'd moved away by then."

"With Jessica's father?"

"I told you before, that didn't work out."

Another avenue of discussion where she'd raised the barricades. "Is it possible Jason is mixed up with this hate group?"

Her incredulous laughter echoed in the enclosed car. "Jason? Are you kidding? Jason's such a flaming liberal, we often wondercd how he ever made it through the Academy background check."

Stephen frowned. "So there's no possibility he's a part of this spider-tattoo brotherhood?"

"Not unless he's their prime target for assassination." Rachel's words flowed freely as long as they circumvented anything personal. Yet she'd shed all her inhibitions last night. Sooner or later she'd have to come clean with him and share the secrets she seemed to guard so fiercely. He vowed to be paticnt. He didn't want to risk doing anything that might make him lose her.

"The hate group has a major score to settle with our Jason," Rachel added.

"The Maitland kidnaping?"

"Jason killed two of their members and, if our suspicions are correct, ruined their hopes for increasing their treasury by a couple million dollars."

Stephen couldn't shake his uneasiness. "Something's been bothering me ever since you first told me about the Maitland case at Uncle George's cabin."

"What?"

He pulled into the left lane to pass a slow RV. "How come Jason burst into that motel room alone where the kidnappers were? Where was his backup?"

"You raised those same questions at the time," she said, apparently unconcerned by his query. "They were all answered at the hearing."

"Hearing?"

"The families of the dead men threatened to sue the Bureau over the deaths of Weed and Bubba," Rachel explained, "but Jason was exonerated by the official investigation, most of which you and I conducted ourselves."

"What did we find out?"

"The evidence was pretty straightforward. Jason received a tip from an informant that Weed and Bubba were holed up in a small motel but preparing to run. Jason called for backup, but, afraid he'd lose them if he waited for help, he drove immediately to their location. When he surprised Weed and Bubba, the kidnapers opened fire on him. Jason returned fire and killed them both."

"Forensic evidence corroborated his story?"

Rachel nodded. "I checked it myself."

"The informant testified about the tip?"

"Yeah. He was an old fisherman who picked up Weed's and Bubba's descriptions off his police radio scanner, saw them enter the motel and called the Bureau."

"You think Maitland could have been involved?" Stephen asked.

"We had those same suspicions at the time, but if Maitland was involved, he hid his tracks without a trace. We never found anything that tied him to the crime."

"What about Milton Carver?"

"The arsonist shot in your custody in Atlanta? What about him?" Rachel asked.

"What if Carver, through his connections with the hate group, had something on Maitland? Maybe Carver figured he could work a deal by fingering Maitland."

"And Maitland had him killed?"

"But maybe not before Carver talked. Why else would I have called you and warned you?" He slammed the heel of his hand against the wheel. "Why can't I *remember?*"

She laid her hand over his fist that was gripping the wheel so tightly his knuckles blanched. "Whether it's members of this hate group or Maitland after us, whoever's on our trail could be after Jason, too. We have to leave a warning at the office so he'll get it when he checks in."

"Okay," Stephen said with a nod. "That's our first item of business."

"And our second?"

"We'll pay another call on Harold Maitland."

ON THEIR WAY into Savannah, Rachel directed Stephen past his old apartment, their favorite restaurants and other local haunts, hoping to jog his memories.

She met with no success. To Stephen, whose handsome face broke into a sweat with his efforts to recall, not even the building where they had worked together for four years seemed familiar.

"The receptionist's name is Marie," Rachel reminded him as they walked from the parking area to the door.

"You take the lead," he said. "We won't tell her about my amnesia or medical leave. She might decide to check with the Atlanta office before cooperating, and Jake and Pete will tell her we're unofficial."

The slender young black woman behind the receptionist's desk did a double take when they entered the office. "I almost didn't recognize y'all in those disguises," she said with a laugh. "What's going on?"

"Undercover work," Rachel answered.

Marie winked. "Undercover? Together? As I remember, that's what we suspected y'all were up to when you worked here."

Rachel ignored Stephen's inquisitive glance and blushed in spite of efforts not to. "Come on, Marie. You know Stephen and I were just good friends."

"Uh-huh." Marie's black eyes twinkled. "And Hurricane Hugo was only a breeze."

To Rachel's relief, Stephen changed the subject. "We need your help, Marie."

The receptionist smiled. "That's why I'm here."

"Can we see the files on the Maitland case?" Stephen asked. "We're checking out the kidnappers' connections to a white supremacist group."

"Our local branch of the Aryan army?" Marie wrinkled her nose. "Rotten bunch. Anything I can do to help shut them down is my pleasure."

Rachel nodded. "Showing us that file will be a good start."

Marie stood and motioned toward the inner office. "There's coffee in the conference room. Help yourselves and I'll bring the file."

An hour and several cups of coffee later, Rachel

stretched and yawned. She and Stephen had filled a legal pad with the names and addresses of Weed's and Bubba's relatives and friends. Checking out each person on the list would be a long and tedious process, but one they were accustomed to. Unlike the glamorous and dangerous versions of FBI life depicted in movies and on television, an agent's routine was primarily this type of grunt work.

They returned the file to Marie's desk as they were leaving.

"Find what you needed?" the receptionist asked.

Stephen shrugged. "Won't know till we conduct a few interviews."

"Anything else I can do?" Marie said.

"There is one thing," Rachel said. "Has Jason Bender checked in lately?"

"No, but he's due to call anytime now."

"Will you give him a message?" Stephen asked.

Marie grabbed a pencil and pad. "Sure."

"Warn him to watch his back," Rachel said. "We suspect that members of this hate group are seeking revenge against the agents involved in the Maitland case. They could be stalking Jason, too."

"Too?" Marie frowned. "They're after you?"

"It's a long story," Rachel said, "and we don't have much time. Just give him the warning, okay?"

"No problem. Y'all be careful."

"We will," Stephen assured her and leaned over her desk. "And, Marie?"

"Yes?"

"If anybody asks, you haven't seen us."

"Then how I'm going to explain this message to Jason?"

"You can tell Jason we've been here," Rachel said, "but please don't mention us to anyone else."

The receptionist folded her arms across her chest and cocked an eyebrow. "Y'all in some kind of trouble?"

"Aside from heading the hate group's hit list?" Rachel said.

Marie nodded sadly. "I see what you mean. That's trouble enough."

"Thanks again, Marie." Stephen grasped Rachel's elbow and steered her toward the door.

"Wait!" Marie called after them.

"What?" Rachel said.

"If Jason wants to talk to you, how can he get in touch?"

"Give him this." Stephen scribbled his cell phone number on a pad on Marie's desk.

They hurried from the building into the dazzling midday sun. A sea breeze carried the autumn smell of burning leaves and the tang of salt marshes, piercing Rachel with nostalgia. For a brief instant she longed to return to the past, to the way things had been when she and Stephen worked together, before they'd made love, but she quickly discarded that desire. To return to the past would mean not having Jessica, and she wouldn't trade her daughter. Not for anything.

She longed to hold her baby, hear her laughter, see her smile. Jessica's absence created an aching hole in her heart. With determination Rachel straightened her shoulders. The sooner they caught the men who pursued them, the sooner she could return to her daughter.

And leave Stephen?

He'd be glad enough to be rid of her after she'd told him the truth about Jessica. She sighed and shoved that unhappy thought to the back of her mind and with it, memories of last night's lovemaking.

"Let's pay that call on the Maitlands," she said in a brisk, all-business tone. "If we can rule out Harold as a suspect, we can concentrate on the white supremacists on our list."

THE SHADY SQUARE that the Maitland house faced was not as crowded as Rachel remembered from a year and a half earlier. Hoopla over the Mercer House, infamous scene of The Book, had evidently subsided, and with it, the crushing tourist trade. The streets and park were almost deserted in the late morning. Only a single horse-drawn carriage conducted sightseers around the square.

A uniformed maid answered the door at the Maitland mansion. "Mr. Maitland isn't in."

"Then we'd like to speak with Mrs. Maitland." Stephen handed the maid his business card.

A few minutes later Margaret Maitland joined them in the drawing room where the maid had asked them to wait. Dressed in designer maternity clothes and with her golden hair elegantly styled, Margaret took one look at them, then hesitated on the threshold in confusion.

"Excuse our disguises," Stephen said. "Part of our job."

Margaret peered more closely, and her expression of disorientation lifted, replaced by a welcoming smile. "Of course, I recognize you now. How nice to see you again. Hardly a day goes by that I don't think of how you saved my life. To what do I owe the honor of this visit?"

"We're in Savannah on another matter," Rachel said, "and wanted to say hello."

"And make sure you haven't had any other scares," Stephen added.

"Scares?"

"No one's tried to kidnap you lately?" Rachel said, smiling to lessen the gravity of the question.

"They wouldn't dare," Margaret said with a glow of contentment. "After that awful day, Harold hired a security service. Now I can't move without a team of bodyguards dogging every step."

Rachel nodded, recalling the burly man in a dark suit reading a magazine on a sofa outside the drawing room. Harold Maitland either wasn't taking any chances or else was putting on a good show of concern.

"I've told Harold there's no need for such measures," Margaret continued, "but he insists. He's grown even more protective with our first child arriving next month. Do you have children, Agent Chandler?"

Margaret hadn't included Rachel in her question, but Rachel wasn't offended. When Stephen was in a room, most women could focus on little else.

"No, I'm not married. But I'd like to have a family of my own one of these days." The surreptitious look he gave Rachel both thrilled and tormented her.

"We want to talk to Harold, too." Rachel quickly changed the topic. "Is he at his office?"

Margaret's smile faded. "He'll be so sorry he missed you. He's been in New York for almost two weeks."

"New York?" Rachel said.

"On behalf of a client. I don't get involved with Harold's work. You know, lawyer-client privilege, confidentiality and all that."

"Will he be home soon?" Stephen asked.

"Not soon enough as far as I'm concerned, what with the baby coming. He's promised to be here for the delivery."

"We won't take any more of your time," Rachel said. "Best wishes to you and your baby."

Back on the street, she turned to Stephen. "How convenient that her husband was out of town when Carver was shot."

Stephen obviously followed her thinking. "But Maitland couldn't have been the man at Uncle George's cabin. Not from the way you described Margaret's husband."

Rachel nodded. "But he could have hired someone to come after us, just like he hired bodyguards for his wife."

"You're right. We can't scratch Maitland from our list of suspects yet."

FOR THE REMAINDER of the morning and into the middle of the afternoon, they attempted to interview

Weed's and Bubba's relatives. A few people slammed doors in their faces, another threatened them with a shotgun if they didn't vacate his property, and none volunteered to answer any questions.

Minnie Fulton, Weed's mother, had shouted obscenities and threatened to loose two ferocious Rottweilers if Rachel and Stephen didn't get off her porch and leave her alone. Without the weight of an official investigation behind them, they had no choice but to comply.

One of Minnie's neighbors, however, proved more cooperative. Driving down the sandy, unpaved road that led from Minnie's house to the highway, they approached another tumbledown shack, perched in an open field between the salt marsh and a pine forest. A stooped old man, checking his mailbox, grinned and waved as they approached.

"Should we stop?" Rachel asked.

"It's worth a try," Stephen said. "His is the only friendly face I've seen since we left Margaret Maitland."

He pulled the Blazer alongside the mailbox and rolled down his window.

"Howdy," the old man, wizened as much by sun and wind as by age, greeted them. "Been to see Minnie?"

"Tried," Stephen said. "She threatened to sic her dogs on us."

The old fellow chuckled and slapped the leg of his faded overalls. "That's Minnie for you. Mean as a snake and twice as low."

"You know the Fultons?" Rachel asked.

"Reckon I do." He grinned again, exposing tobacco-stained teeth. "Lived next door to 'em over fifty years."

"We're investigating the circumstances of Weed Fulton's death," Stephen explained and showed his federal ID. "Would you mind answering a few questions, Mr—?"

"Kincaid, Thomas Kincaid, but most folks just call me Old Tom. Come up to the house and sit a spell. We don't get much company in these parts, and I been mighty lonesome since my wife died."

Rachel and Stephen followed Old Tom up a dirt path, swept clean and lined with seashells. Chickens pecked among the frostbitten grass of the yard, and an ancient coonhound, sleeping in a puddle of sun on the porch, raised its head and considered them with sad eyes and drooping jowls before resuming his nap.

Tom waved them into rocking chairs on the porch and perched on the rail in front of them. "What do you need to know?"

"Tell us about Minnie Fulton," Rachel said.

Tom scowled. "I knowed Minnie since she was knee-high to a grasshopper. Always was a ornery cuss. And her sons was just as bad."

"Sons?" Stephen said. "Weed had brothers?"

"Weed?" Tom turned and spat over the rail, as if he had a bad taste in his mouth. "His Christian name was Arthur, but they called him Weed, 'cause he was so wild."

"Weed's brothers?" Rachel prodded.

"Ralph Fulton is the youngest," Tom said, shaking

his head. "He's a strange one. Left home a few years back. Lives in the Okefenokee Swamp. Rumor is he's running drugs outta Florida. Served Minnie right when Milton moved in with Ralph, leaving her alone."

"Milton?" Stephen said. "Milton Fulton?"

Old Tom grinned. "Milton's the oldest son. No one knows who his daddy is—not even Minnie—so he goes by his mother's maiden name, Carver."

"You hadn't heard?" Rachel asked. "Milton Carver was murdered in Atlanta."

Old Tom nodded. "Not surprised. All them boys'll come to bad ends. I knowed it since they were young'uns."

"What can you tell us about Fulton, Minnie's husband?" Stephen said.

"Dead. Nigh onto ten years now. Minnie swore he died in a hunting accident, but wouldn't surprise me none if she and those worthless boys shot him."

"Nice family," Stephen said with a grimace. "Tell me more about Ralph."

Old Tom shuddered. "You don't want to mess with Ralph. He's even meaner than his ma."

"Can you tell us where to find him?" Rachel asked.

"I reckon I can remember. Only went into the swamp once, when I helped Ralph move outta his Ma's house and carried some of his stuff in my pickup. Course, now he's got a truck of his own. Bright red. You can see it coming a mile away."

Red, Stephen thought, just like the pickup that had

arrived at Uncle George's cabin with its Magnum-toting driver.

"I'll get a map from the car," Stephen said, "so you can show us where Ralph lives."

Two hours later the Blazer was slogging through the Okefenokee on their way to find Ralph Fulton.

"It's a good thing we're in an SUV," Rachel said, "or we'd never make it through these waterlogged roads."

"If the water gets much deeper, we'll wish we had an airboat."

He grinned at Rachel, admiring her loveliness before returning his attention to the almost nonexistent road. More and more, his memories were resurfacing. He'd recognized Margaret Maitland and her house on the square. But most powerful were the memories and emotions that revolved around the woman in the car beside him. He had loved her, without doubt. Being with her now, returning to the working partnership they had enjoyed for so many years made him want to run and shout in exhilaration.

But he'd have to wait until the killers who stalked them were caught before he could relax enough to enjoy his newfound happiness.

He drove slowly around a curve. Directly ahead a hillock of land, surrounded by moss-draped cypress that blocked the sunlight, rose out of the murky water. At its center stood a tin-roofed shack on four-foot stilts. Parked beside the entrance was a red pickup, the same make and model Stephen had noted at the mountain cabin.

Stephen cut the Blazer's engine and drew his gun.

"Guard the front while I circle the rear. Ralph may have a boat out back."

"Stephen—"

"Yes?"

"Be careful."

He leaned across the console that divided the seats and kissed her lightly on the lips. "Take care, Doc. I don't want anything happening to you."

He slipped from the car and ran at a crouch through the covering cypress to the rear of the shack. A flat-bottomed boat with a high-powered motor was tied to a makeshift dock. He had stepped into the boat to disable the motor, when Rachel's call broke the stillness.

"Stephen, you'd better come here."

Her voice relayed an urgency that sent his stomach into free fall. Had Ralph gotten a drop on her? He scrambled from the boat and cautiously circled back to the front of the shack. Rachel stood alone on the porch.

She nodded toward the open door. "Take a look."

He climbed the rickety steps. What greeted his vision first were the worn soles of a pair of boots just inside the door. As he stepped across the threshold, a body stared up at him, a bullet hole between the dead eyes.

Chapter Twelve

"Is it Ralph Fulton?" Rachel asked behind him.

Stephen removed a wallet from the dead man's jeans and searched through its contents. "That's the name on the license, and the photo is a match."

"I don't understand," Rachel said. "If Ralph Fulton was after *us,* who killed him? And why?"

"We need some answers instead of more questions." Frustrated, Stephen removed his cell phone from his pocket and dialed information for the number of the nearest law enforcement agency.

An hour later, as the dark swamp reverberated with the noise of crickets and frogs and the bass rumbles of bull gators, the sheriff's crime scene unit surveyed the murder site beneath the harsh glare of artificial lights.

Stephen finished relating his account of their investigation of Ralph Fulton to a sheriff's detective, and Rachel, who'd been talking to one of the technicians, joined him.

He curved his arm over her shoulder. "The sheriff

says we're free to go. I've told them all we know."
He led her toward the car.

"The technician found a .22 cartridge on the
porch." Rachel said, snuggling against his side and
shivering in the swamp's damp cold. "Fulton must
have been shot the instant he opened the door."

"Out here in the middle of nowhere," Stephen said
thoughtfully, scratching his chin, "it's odd he wasn't
holding a weapon. He apparently knew his visitor."

"A .22 caused that wound in your left arm," Rachel reminded him.

Stephen noted the worry in her eyes and wished he
could somehow make all her problems disappear.
"It's possible whoever killed Ralph is the same person who shot me. Any other evidence?"

"No tire tracks or footprints. The recent rains destroyed them." She was all business, and his admiration swelled. Despite being apart from her daughter—or perhaps because of her eagerness to put an
end to that separation—she had been relentless from
the beginning of the investigation in tracking every
clue. "There's nothing significant in the shack except
some flyers and propaganda used by the hate group."

Stephen opened the door of the Blazer for Rachel
to climb inside, then circled the vehicle and slid into
the driver's seat.

"Are you thinking what I'm thinking?" she asked
as he started the engine.

"If the hate group is after us, why are they the ones
turning up dead?"

"Exactly. Somebody hired Weed and Bubba to kill
Margaret Maitland. When they bungled the job, who-

ever it was tipped us off so we'd catch them. Ralph Fulton and Milton Carver are both related to Weed. Now they're dead, too. Everything points back somehow to the Maitland kidnapping.''

Stephen turned the headlights on high beam to illuminate the pitch-dark road. ''There's only one problem with that theory. Why wasn't the mastermind behind the kidnapping afraid Weed and Bubba would identify him?''

Rachel thought for a moment. ''Maybe Weed and Bubba never knew who he was. Maybe he wore a disguise and used a false name when he met with them. Or he could have hired them through an intermediary and they never laid eyes on him.''

''Then why were Milton Carver and Ralph Fulton killed?''

''Maybe *they* were the intermediaries,'' Rachel said, ''and the person behind the kidnapping wanted them silenced for good.''

Stephen considered her suggestion. ''If Milton and Ralph were the intermediaries, they could have been blackmailing the mastermind.''

''But why would the person behind the kidnapping want you and me dead?''

Stephen relished the familiar give-and-take, recalling other crimes they'd solved together as several flashes of memory returned. ''Maybe he feared Carver had confessed to me in Atlanta.''

''If that's the case, why drag me into it?''

''Could be revenge, pure and hateful. We're the ones who found Margaret, helped her identify Weed and Bubba, and ruined the whole scheme.''

In the dim light from the dashboard, he could see Rachel shaking her head. "I don't like this. The person with the most to gain from Margaret Maitland's death was her husband. Now she's only weeks away from having their first child. I'd hate to have to tell her that her husband and the father of her baby was willing to kill her for her money."

At the anguish in her tone, Stephen stopped the vehicle, turned toward her and took her hand. "First thing tomorrow we'll contact Maitland's office and find out where he's staying in New York. We'll get to the bottom of this."

She sighed in frustration. "What if Maitland's New York alibi is solid?"

"That won't mean he's not guilty. He could have hired others to do his dirty work, just like the kidnapping. If he did, we'll find them. I'm tired of being the hunted in his cat-and-mouse game."

She looked through the windshield, peering into the darkness. "Why did you stop the car?"

He drew her against his chest and tightened his arms around her. She smelled so good, felt so right. "Because there's something I have to do right now, something I've been wanting to do all day." He unfastened his seat belt, glided his fingers across her shoulders, down the length of her arms and tipped her face toward him.

She came willingly into his embrace and lifted her arms around his neck. Her curves conformed to him with the effortless ease of remembrance, sparking every cell in his body with exquisite need. This perfect fit had been imprinted on his mind, and he never wanted to let her go. Tangling his fingers in her hair, he kissed her, reveling in the sweet, familiar taste of her.

Her response was immediate. With a soft moan she caressed his shoulders, urging him closer, offering him a safe haven in a storm of need.

Minutes later he raised his head. "Solving this case is more important to me than ever now."

"Why?" Her eyes sparkled in the dim light, and her voice was breathless, skewering him with renewed desire.

"I want to marry you, Doc. I want you and Jessica and me to be a family."

An ominous stillness descended on her, and the light went out in her eyes. "That's...not possible."

Confusion broadsided him. She'd said she loved him. He'd felt it in her kiss. Had he read everything wrong, including his memories of her?

"As much as I love you," he argued, "anything's possible."

She pushed away and avoided his eyes. "There're too many things you don't remember. Too much about me you never knew in the first place."

He grasped her chin and gently turned her face toward him. "I know one thing for sure. There's nothing you can tell me that will make me stop loving you, Doc."

"Don't." She pressed her fingers against his lips. "Don't make promises you can't keep."

He covered her hand with his, kissed each of her fingertips and flashed her a reassuring smile. "We can clear this up right now. Tell me what I should know, then I'll prove how much I love you.''

She drew away, her eyes misting with tears. ''It isn't that easy.''

Wrapping his arms around her, he pulled her back against his chest and stroked her hair. ''Sure it is. Just say the words. I'm listening.''

''Will you do me a favor first?''

''Anything.''

''Will you kiss me one last time?''

''I'll gladly kiss you, Doc, but believe me, it won't be the last.''

She lifted her lips to his, kissing him with a fierceness that fired his blood again. Surrendering to desire, he abandoned all conscious thought, exploring the planes and contours of her back, the swell of her breasts, the curve of her thighs.

With a sweet reluctance she pulled away. ''I'd better tell you now before I lose my courage.''

''I'm listening.'' He smiled again to encourage her, thinking nothing she could tell him was as grave as her expression suggested.

''After I graduated from medical school,'' she began, ''I was supposed to marry Brad, whom I'd known since I was three. Our families were close, we had dated through high school and college, and everyone expected us to marry.''

Her hands fluttered nervously in her lap. He placed his over them to still them. ''Relax. Just tell me. Then everything will be okay.''

The grief in her eyes indicated she didn't believe him, and an uneasiness began to gnaw at his confidence. Had he been wrong to trust her, to love her? He shoved the unsettling question aside. The way he felt about her now, nothing could shake his love for her.

She took a deep breath and plunged ahead into her story. "The wedding was supposed to be the social event of the summer in Raleigh. My parents had spared no expense, and Brad's folks had planned a huge reception at the country club. I was standing in the church vestibule with Dad, waiting to walk down the aisle, when Brad's best man delivered the note."

"Note?"

"Brad had run away. At the eleventh hour, he'd found the strength to admit he didn't love me, that he'd asked me to marry him because everyone expected it, but he didn't have the courage to tell me face-to-face."

"Did you love him?" Stephen asked gently.

"At the time I thought I did." She met his gaze, and her smile was bittersweet. "Now I know what real love is."

He resisted the urge to kiss her again. Telling her story was an obvious and painful effort, and she needed to get whatever was bothering her off her conscience.

Gently he prodded her. "What happened next?"

"The wedding was canceled, of course. At the time I thought my heart was broken, my life ruined. Looking back, I realize I was more humiliated than hurt. I threw myself into my FBI training and never looked back."

"Never?"

She shook her head. "And I vowed I would never allow anyone to hurt me the way Brad did."

"I can understand your feelings, but that's not such a terrible secret. Knowing it certainly doesn't make me love you less."

"That's not the secret," she said softly with a look of such agony that it made him want to cry. "I told you that same story years ago. It's only background."

At her pained expression, his throat tightened with a premonition that her story was about to take a turn he wouldn't like. "Then you'd better tell me the rest."

"When I came to Savannah, I was assigned as your partner. For four years we worked well together, and I thought we were just good friends—"

"Brother and sister, you said."

She nodded, and even in the dimness of the dashboard lights, he could see her blush.

"Several times you asked me to marry you," she said, "but I always thought you were teasing. I didn't realize that in my efforts to forget the pain Brad had caused me, I'd closed off my emotions so effectively that I couldn't recognize my own feelings, much less anyone else's."

"You shouldn't blame yourself. That's a natural protective response."

"But it caused a lot of trouble—and a horrible mistake."

"What kind of mistake?"

She shuddered. "I'm getting ahead of myself. I already told you about our lovemaking the night of your going-away party. Until recently, I'd convinced myself that it happened because we'd had too much to drink.''

''What really happened?'' His sense of uneasiness grew. He loved her, and he didn't want her to tell him anything that might shake that love.

Tears pooled in her eyes and slipped down her cheeks. ''You loved me. I can see it now.''

''And you?''

''I loved you, too. I was just too afraid of being hurt again to admit it. So after the party, I wouldn't take your calls or see you again. I convinced myself that we would both be too embarrassed by what had happened, and I didn't want to spoil the memories of our friendship with regrets about that…uncomfortable encounter.''

Stephen shifted uneasily. ''So I left for Atlanta without seeing you again?''

''You tried.'' She forced a weak smile through her tears. ''You almost wore out my phone with your calls, and you came by my apartment, but I never answered the phone or the door.''

''I just moved to Atlanta, and you never heard from me again? I should be the one with the guilty conscience.''

''Please.'' She laid her hand on his arm. ''Don't make this harder by trying to take the blame.''

Relief blew through him like a sea breeze. She'd been tormenting herself over a simple misunderstanding. ''Sounds like there's blame enough to go around on both sides. Maybe we should just forget it ever happened and start over.''

"There's more." Her voice was so soft he struggled to hear her.

"More?" His apprehension returned.

"Three months after you left, Jason told me you'd met a woman in Atlanta—"

"Anne Michelle?"

She nodded. "And you were going to be married."

"I remember all that. And I told you I only *thought* I loved her. What drew me to her all along was that she reminded me of you."

"What you don't know," Rachel said quickly, as if afraid she'd lose her nerve if she hesitated, "is that the same day I heard about your engagement, I discovered I was pregnant with Jessica."

He blinked in confusion. "You've lost me. When did Jessica's father enter the picture?"

She raised her head and looked at him with eyes filled with guilt and tears. "*You* are Jessica's father."

It took a few seconds for that fact to sink in. When it did, emotions swamped him.

Astonishing joy.

Incredible pride.

And burning anger.

"I have a daughter, and you never told me?"

"You were getting married. I didn't want to jeopardize your happiness. Or make you feel obligated to me."

Conflicting emotions battled within him. In his furor at her for not telling him about his daughter, he wanted to smash something. He also wanted to climb out of the truck and dance for joy.

He had a *daughter*.

How could she hide such a thing from him? "I had a *right* to know!"

"I can see that now," she said. "I don't blame you if your feelings for me aren't the same now as they were before I told you."

"But—"

The cell phone in his pocket rang, but he ignored it.

"Your phone," she murmured.

"Forget it." It wasn't every day a man became a father. He wanted time to banish his anger, to savor the moment.

"It might be Jason."

Regretfully, because he had so much he wanted to say to her, so many questions to ask, he answered the call.

"May I speak with Rachel?" a strange male voice said.

Stephen handed her the phone.

"For me?" she said with a puzzled look at Stephen.

He nodded.

"This is Rachel," she spoke into the phone.

As she listened, Stephen watched the blood leave her face. She began to tremble.

"Don't worry, Dad," Rachel finally said. "We're on our way."

"Jessica?" Stephen asked when she switched off the phone. "Is she ill?"

Rachel shook her head, her eyes glowing with panic. "She's been kidnapped."

Chapter Thirteen

Jessica, kidnapped!

The killer who stalked them had her baby. Fear and guilt roiled through Rachel like acid, until she feared she would faint from the pain.

"I never should have left her," she said, fighting the hysteria that inundated her in waves. Stephen's anger at her deception seemed small compared to the risk to her daughter's life.

Stephen grabbed her by the shoulders and shook her. When he spoke, his voice was stern. "Wallowing in guilt won't get Jessica back. Tell me what your father said."

Stephen's example of putting personal feelings aside helped. She had watched him struggle between fury and elation when she broke the news of his daughter.

And now that daughter had been stolen from her bed.

She sucked in a deep breath to steady herself. "Mrs. Kidbrough put Jessica to bed after dinner, then went to check on her a little while ago. She wasn't in her crib. Before they could call the police, the phone rang.''

''A ransom demand?''

Fighting back tears, she nodded. ''A man. Dr. Kidbrough didn't recognize the voice. The kidnapper warned if they contacted the police or the FBI, he'd...kill Jessica.''

Stephen swore under his breath. ''How much ransom does he want?''

''He doesn't want money. He wants us.'' She raised her gaze to his. Misery swam in his dark eyes, deep lines edged his generous mouth, and his forehead wrinkled, as if in pain. He looked as devastated as she felt.

He slammed his fist against the steering wheel. ''It's our stalker. He's using Jessica as bait to draw us to him, the stinking coward. What type of human being places the life of a child in danger?''

''The same kind who murdered Milton Carver and Ralph Fulton.'' Rachel could no longer hold back the tears. Sobs racked her body, and she ached to hold her baby. That someone wanted to kill Rachel seemed insignificant compared to someone putting Jessica in danger. If anything happened to her daughter, even if Rachel survived, emotionally she would be as good as dead.

Was the kidnapper keeping her baby warm? Calming her fears? Was Jessica frightened, crying for her mother?

''If Harold Maitland's behind this,'' Stephen threatened through gritted teeth, ''when I get my hands on him, he'll wish he'd never been born.''

Remembering the rest of her father's message, Rachel scrubbed the tears from her cheeks with the back of her hand. "We'd better get moving. We're supposed to be at the I-85 rest area at the Georgia-South Carolina line by midnight."

"The kidnapper said he'd bring Jessica there?"

Rachel shook her head. "He said we're to wait by the public phones for a call that will give us instructions."

"I know that rest area," Stephen said with a frown. "It's surrounded by rolling, wooded hills, the perfect spot for an ambush."

"I have to be there," Rachel insisted. "I have to get Jessica back, no matter what the risk."

"I know." He pulled her close. "But that doesn't mean we have to go alone."

She jerked from his embrace. "What are you saying?"

"We'll alert the FBI. Have them comb the rest area before we arrive."

"No! He threatened to kill her if we brought in anyone else."

Stephen started the car and headed along the dark, waterlogged road toward the highway.

"You've handled enough of these kidnapping cases, Doc." The gentleness in his voice generated fresh tears. "You know the statistics. Jessica will have a better chance of coming through unhurt if we notify the authorities now."

Her intellect warred with her emotions. Her head knew Stephen was right, but her heart wanted to trust the kidnapper not to harm Jessica if Rachel did as he asked.

But Jessica was Stephen's daughter, too.

"We can't take that chance. Don't forget that Jessica is *your* daughter—"

"*I* won't forget," he said sharply, "although it may take some time to get used to that fact."

Rachel ignored the sarcasm in his tone. "And you still think we should risk calling in the Bureau?"

He hesitated only slightly before nodding. "We're several hours' drive from the rest area. A phone call now to Jack and Pete in the Atlanta office will mobilize the FBI and their resources. They can be in place at the rest stop before we get there."

Rachel struggled for objectivity. She couldn't help Jessica if she didn't think straight, so she forced herself to set aside the risk factor and consider the advantages of Stephen's suggestion. "Jack and Pete can set up a phone tap so we can pinpoint the kidnapper's location."

Stephen slowed for a stretch of deeper water on the swampy road. "And they can arrange for teams to scour the rest area and its surroundings to flush out a sniper. Otherwise, we'll be easy targets for someone with a night-vision scope and high-powered rifle."

He pressed the accelerator and sped down the dark road, and the Blazer threw sheets of water in its wake. Rachel watched the lines tighten around his eyes and tried to swallow against the choking guilt that blocked her throat. Guilt at not being there when her daughter needed her, guilt at not telling Stephen about Jessica. He hadn't known he had a daughter, and now, before he'd had a chance to know and love his child, the kidnapper might—

Stop it! Don't even think it!

She gave herself a mental shake and assured herself that Jessica would be all right. They'd rescue her, just as they had Margaret Maitland.

But Margaret Maitland almost died, an inner voice taunted her. *And your childhood friend Caroline. No one saved her.*

She forced the terrifying thoughts from her mind and tried to concentrate on something else. She recalled Stephen's reaction when she'd told him he was Jessica's father. She'd seen anger tense his muscles, spark in his eyes. Before her confession, he'd promised to love her, no matter what she told him.

"Stephen?" Her voice shook with apprehension. She needed his love now more than ever.

"Yes?"

She reached deep inside for courage. "Can you forgive me for keeping Jessica a secret from you?"

He didn't take his eyes off the road, and his expression remained fixed, hard. "Let's deal with one thing at a time. Our first priority is getting Jessica back."

"You're right, of course." Rachel slumped in her seat. Rescuing her daughter was all that mattered. She would deal with a broken heart after Jessica was safe in her arms.

STEPHEN HUNG UP the pay phone outside the gas station where the swamp road met the highway and returned to the Blazer.

Rachel looked at him expectantly as he climbed into the driver's seat. The terror in her green eyes, the pallor of her face and the nervous quiver in her hands made him want to grab her close and affirm that everything would turn out fine. But he couldn't allow his emotions to interfere with the job he had to do.

And he couldn't mislead her.

Even if they rescued Jessica, a more than equal chance existed that one or both of them might be hurt, even killed. The only way to protect himself and Rachel was to keep his feelings buttoned down. If he gave in to his fears of losing Rachel and the daughter he'd barely known, they were all lost.

"Did you reach them?" Rachel asked.

He turned the key in the ignition and pulled onto the highway. "Jack is putting things into motion. Everything will be in place by the time we get there. Surveillance, phone taps..."

"Assault teams?"

"Those, too." He'd left them out on purpose, not wanting her to envision a scenario where such deadly force would be needed, but she'd been with the Bureau too long not to recall procedure.

"Good." She leaned back against the seat. "We may need a little help from our friends."

"I also asked Jack to have the New York office check out Harold Maitland's movements and contacts over the past two weeks."

No matter how much she tried to suppress her fear, thinking straight was difficult. This wasn't just another case. Her baby's life was at stake.

"With Fulton dead," she said, "Maitland's our only lead. Let's hope the New York office turns up something."

They drove in silence until they reached the Savannah office, where Agent Stan Lewolsky provided them with bullet-proof vests and headgear. Stan walked outside with them and waited while Stephen stowed the equipment in the back of the car.

"Thanks for your help," he told Stan.

"No problem," the agent said, extending his hand. "Good luck. And take care of our Rachel. She's pretty special to us in this office."

Stephen gripped Stan's hand. "She's special to me, too."

Stephen slid into the driver's seat, and Stan circled the car to Rachel's window. He squeezed Rachel's hand, resting on the window frame. "If anyone can get your baby back, the Bureau can."

"I know," Rachel said, "and I appreciate your help."

"Look out for yourself." Stan released her hand.

"Did Stephen ask you about Jason?" Rachel asked.

The agent nodded. "Marie's been waiting for him to check in, but we haven't heard from him."

"I hope he's all right."

Stan's grin split his freckled, sunburned face. "Jason's in the same league with you two. He can take care of himself."

"You think Stan's right?" Rachel asked Stephen as they drove away.

"About what?"

"About Jason taking care of himself."

He frowned. "Staying safe is one thing if you know someone's after you. It's another if you have no idea you're being hunted."

He heard her breath catch in her throat. "So Jason could already be...just like Ralph Fulton."

He silently cursed himself for frightening her. "The Appalachian Trail is remote, rugged and hundreds of miles long. Tracking Jason in that extended wilderness would be almost impossible."

"You're right." Her expression brightened. "Besides, Jason always chafed against rules and regulations. As I recall, he was never punctual about checking in during his other hiking vacations."

They lapsed into silence again, lost in their own thoughts, and remained quiet as the Blazer ate up the miles between them and the rest area on the Georgia-South Carolina border. The clock on the dashboard ticked away the hours to their midnight rendezvous, and the temperature gauge above the windshield recorded the dropping degrees.

By the time they stopped at a rest area closest to their destination, the temperature had fallen into the teens. Rachel shivered when she removed her jacket to don the bullet-proof Kevlar vest.

"I hope he's keeping Jessica warm," she said.

The anxiety in her voice pierced through him, sharper than the cold. He shrugged into his vest, put on his jacket, and handed her a hard hat on which the distinctive neon letters FBI had been covered with black tape.

"Keep this on," he ordered, "no matter what."

She appeared small and fragile in the protective gear, and memories inundated him of Rachel on other missions, clad in bullet-proof vest and headgear, weapon drawn, the lines of her beautiful face set with purpose. She'd carried her weight and more in every operation, no matter how dangerous. She might look delicate, but she was tough and competent. He could count on Doc to back him up and see this through.

For the first time since she'd related the call from her father, Stephen felt confident that the two of them—no, make that the three of them—would come through this in one piece.

He adjusted the strap on her headgear. "Ready?"

She jutted her chin forward with a determination that touched his heart and nodded. "Ready."

Less than fifteen minutes later they arrived at the rest area the kidnapper had designated. Stephen slowed the Blazer as it left the highway and drove cautiously into the lit parking area.

Even close to midnight, the interstate rest stop was far from deserted. Several eighteen-wheelers and a few recreational vehicles were parked in the open lot. Hidden in one of them, the assault team waited, suited up and armed, ready to respond in seconds.

At the refreshment stand, a couple operated the coffee machine, and Stephen wondered if they were agents, already in place. A man, smoking a cigarette, lolled in the shadows near the rest rooms. Another read the headlines from a newspaper rack. In the shadow of the trees at the far end of the parking area, another man sat in a car.

Any one of the strangers could be another agent.

Or the kidnapper, waiting to place a call on his cell phone. Stephen pulled into the parking space nearest the pay phone and stopped. The clock indicated five minutes until midnight.

"This is it," he said. "Keep your head down in case there's a sniper out there."

She nodded, her face grim. "Let's hope the agents here have already done a thermal scan of the woods and eliminated that problem."

She looked so worried, in spite of his vow to remain objective, he leaned over and kissed her quickly on the lips. "Everything's going to be okay."

Before she had a chance to respond, he was out of the car and strolling toward the phone. It began to ring before he reached it.

Stephen sprinted the last few feet and grabbed the receiver.

"Chandler?" a familiar male voice asked.

"Who are you?"

"You know damned well who I am. I drilled a hole in you a few days back."

Stephen had heard the voice before but couldn't place it. Maybe he recalled it only from his previous encounter with the gunman. "I've had a touch of amnesia since then. Can't remember much of anything."

"That's good—if it's true. If you can't remember who I am, then you haven't blabbed about me to anyone else."

"What's to blab?" Stephen knew the longer he kept the man talking, the better chance the listening agents had of tracing the call.

"Is Rachel with you?" the kidnapper asked.

"She's in the car. Do you want her to come to the phone?"

The man on the other end of the line laughed. "That would be a good delaying tactic, wouldn't it? Give your buddies listening in a longer time to track me. Well, it won't work. I've routed this call six ways to Sunday. I could talk for an hour before the tracer could unravel all the relays."

"Where's Jessica?" Stephen demanded. "Is she all right?"

"She's fine." The kidnapper paused with a significance that sent a chill down Stephen's back. "For now."

"What do you mean, 'for now'? What do we have to do to get the baby back?"

"First, call off the Bureau."

"What are you talking about?" Stephen bluffed.

"That rest area is crawling with agents. I saw them myself earlier. I warned you, Chandler. I should kill the kid—"

"No! Just tell me what you want us to do."

"What guarantee do I have that you'll lose the Feds?"

"The same guarantee I have that you won't harm Jessica if we do as you say."

The kidnapper laughed again, a rasping sound that irritated Stephen's ears. "You're sharp, Chandler. Always had a peculiar way of homing in on the truth."

"What do you want?"

"Lose the Feds. Then drive straight to that cabin on the mountaintop outside Glenville."

"The place you trashed?"

"That's the one. Both of you'd better be there—
alone—in two hours or the kid's dead. Understand?"

"I understand, but—" Stephen saved his breath.
He was talking to an empty line.

He walked back to the Blazer and raised his hand
to signal the watching agents.

RACHEL PEERED through the windshield at the mountain road, illuminated only by the high beam of the
headlights. Stephen was pushing the Blazer as fast as
he could and still maintain control on the dangerous
curves, but the vehicle seemed to crawl.

A little more than an hour ago, over the objections
of the special agent in charge, she and Stephen had
asked the FBI to withdraw.

Stephen had already explained to her the caller's
demands. "It's a trap," he added. "There's no other
way to look at it."

"It's our only chance of getting Jessica back safe.
We'll have to do it the kidnapper's way."

"You're sure? He could have friends at the cabin.
We could be outnumbered."

"We're trained agents," she said, terrified in spite
of her brave words. "We'll have the advantage."

Now, as they passed through the tiny resort town
of Cashiers just miles from Glenville, she steeled herself for the encounter. She glanced at Stephen beside
her, his handsome face set in grim lines. If she had
to risk her life, she could think of no one else better
as backup. They'd faced danger together many times
before, and knowing his skill and coolheadedness
comforted her.

Stephen surprised her by turning off the main highway that led to the road to his uncle's cabin.

"Where are you going?"

"The kidnapper will see us coming if we take the
main road," he said. "We'll use the old logging road
that starts at Clayton Jones's farm."

She nodded in agreement. If they could sneak up
on the cabin, they could assess the situation and
maybe even surprise the kidnapper.

Stephen parked the vehicle at the curve where Rachel had waited for him when they'd fled the cabin a
few days ago. A few days that had seemed like a
lifetime. He checked his watch. "We have time to
climb the rest of the way on foot and still make our
deadline. Otherwise he'll hear the car coming.
Ready?"

Rachel nodded and exited the car.

Together they ascended the road, following the trail
Rachel's Explorer had broken through the overgrown
brush a few days earlier. She stumbled once, and Stephen reached down to pull her to her feet.

He was all business, concentrating on their task at
hand, and she couldn't help but wonder when this was
all over—if they both survived—what his feelings for
her would be. The news of Jessica's kidnapping had
come hard on the heels of Rachel's confession. Stephen hadn't had time to assimilate what she'd told
him, much less decide how he felt about it.

About her.

She had bungled everything. For Stephen, for Jessica and for herself. The thought of how things might
have been stabbed her with a sharp sense of loss.

The best she could hope for now was to rescue her daughter. She might have to face life without Stephen, but she couldn't endure anything happening to her child.

Winded from their climb, they reached the edge of the clearing. No lights shone in the back rooms of the cabin.

Please, God, she prayed, *let Jessica be asleep inside one of those bedrooms, safe and unharmed.*

Stephen touched her arm and motioned for her to follow. At a crouch, he moved silently through the shrubs and bushes on the edge of the clearing until he'd circled to the front of the cabin. He dropped to a prone position, and Rachel flattened herself in the dead leaves beside him.

A red pickup was parked out front. Light streamed from the living room windows onto the front porch, but no one moved in the main room.

Suddenly, something moved in the shadows of the porch. A man stepped forward and peered down the mountain toward the main road. With a sigh of exasperation, he settled onto the top step and placed a revolver across his knees.

Light from the room fell across his profile, and Rachel bit her lip to suppress an exclamation of surprise.

The kidnapper was Jason Bender.

STEPHEN HEARD RACHEL'S quick intake of breath, and when the man on the porch leaned into the light, he recognized his face. Memories associated with that face flooded him, but the name eluded him.

Rachel wriggled closer and placed her lips against

his ear. "It's Jason Bender," she whispered so softly the words were almost imperceptible.

Bender.

When he put the name with the face, every memory returned. Jason Bender had been his friend. Together they'd spent hundreds of competitive hours on the racquetball courts, driven to Atlanta where they had season tickets for the Braves home games, bent elbows over imported beer swapping stories of previous assignments.

Once, when Jason had drunk more than usual, he'd launched into the story of his childhood, growing up as the only child of a divorced mother, driven to embitterment and perpetual anger over her desertion by her husband. She had cleaned other people's houses to raise him, but also had managed to implant in him the unshakable conviction that he was better than others and destined for greatness.

Jason had strived to achieve the success his mother had prophesied, but he'd run into obstacles, living beyond his means with a mountain of credit card debt and taking shortcuts and chances on his job that caused the Bureau to pass over him time and again with promotions and accolades.

Jason had gradually turned bitter and withdrawn, so changed from the friend Stephen had originally known that it seemed a stranger, not Jason, had shot him in Atlanta.

And threatened to murder Rachel.

With the complete return of Stephen's memories came a deeper appreciation of how much he loved the woman at his side. When she'd walked out without saying goodbye the morning after his going-away party, he'd been desperate to talk to her, to tell her how much she meant to him. To ask her to marry him.

When she'd avoided him and refused to answer her phone, he'd assumed he'd overstepped his bounds in making love to her and ruined any chance he'd had. He had hoped to marry Rachel and take her to Atlanta with him. When he went alone, he felt as if all the purpose had drained out of his life. He'd done his job, but without Rachel to give meaning to his life, he'd only gone through the motions.

On the rebound, he'd met Anne Michelle Logan in Atlanta. But Anne Michelle, while reminding him of Rachel, wasn't the Doc he loved. By the time he'd realized that and broken off with Anne Michelle, he'd heard rumors Rachel had met someone and had had a child. He felt as devastated as if he'd lost her all over again.

If only he'd known she'd had *his* child, that knowledge would have saved them both so much loneliness and heartache. Now nothing mattered except Rachel, Jessica and their happiness. And when he settled the score with Jason Bender…

Jason's actions had effectively killed any friendship Stephen had ever felt for him. He intended to see that the rogue agent paid for his crimes, paid most of all for terrorizing Rachel and her little girl.

His little girl.

After signaling to Rachel to cover him, he maneuvered quietly through the woods to the side of the building and sprinted across the darkly shadowed lawn to the far edge of the porch. Silently he climbed over the rail and approached Jason from behind.

With his anger tamped under rigid control, he placed the barrel of his automatic against the back of Jason's neck. "Drop the gun, Bender."

At the edge of the clearing, Rachel rose to her feet and advanced to the cabin, her gun also aimed at Jason.

Stephen grabbed Jason's Magnum. "Watch him," he said to Rachel, "while I check the cabin."

A brief sweep of the rooms revealed the place was empty. He returned to the porch. "There's no one here."

"No one?" Rachel's face was pinched and white in the dim light. "Where's Jessica?"

Stephen longed to comfort her, but he didn't dare take his concentration from Jason. As Stephen now vividly recalled, the man knew every trick in the book.

"You'll never find her," Jason said with satisfaction.

Rachel went rigid with fear. "She isn't..."

"Dead?" Jason's evil laugh made Stephen shiver. "Not yet. I left her hidden at the base of some rocks on the mountain. She's bundled up pretty good, but I'd guess in about an hour hypothermia will begin to set in and..." His words trailed off significantly.

Stephen had to exercise every ounce of self-control to keep from hitting Jason. What kind of monster abandoned a baby in the wilderness, in below-freezing weather?

"Tell us where she is," Rachel pleaded. "Let me find her and I'll do anything you want."

"You'll let me go?" Sarcasm edged the agent's voice.

"You know we can't do that," Stephen said. "But the court will go a lot easier on you without a charge of infant homicide added to your crimes."

Rachel raced toward the porch, gun drawn.

Close by, the excited bark of a dog broke the stillness. Distracted, she turned toward the sound.

In a blur of unexpected movement, Jason yanked a gun from an ankle holster, lunged at Rachel and fired point-blank.

"No-o-o!" Stephen's scream echoed off the surrounding hill.

The bullet struck Rachel squarely in the chest, knocking her to the ground.

Chapter Fourteen

"Drop the gun, Bender," Stephen yelled, torn between rushing to Rachel and apprehending her assailant.

Jason pivoted, turning the weapon on Stephen. "You're not taking me alive. Either I kill you or you shoot me."

Jason raised his weapon until it pointed between Stephen's eyes. The rogue agent's finger flexed on the trigger.

"Give it up." Stephen thought fast. He couldn't risk shooting Jason. Only he knew where Jessica was hidden. "If Rachel or I don't check in within the next five minutes, this mountain will be swarming with FBI and sheriff's deputies. You'll never get away."

He exhaled in relief and edged toward Rachel when Jason relaxed his trigger finger.

"I'm not going to jail," Jason said, his face contorted with anger and fear. "My mother always called my father a jailbird. I won't be like him."

"Just give me the gun," Stephen said, "and tell me where you hid the baby. Then we'll sort this all out in Atlanta." He used every bit of self-control to keep from pulling the trigger and blowing Jason away for what he'd done to Rachel. The sight of her still, crumpled form filled Stephen with warring emotions of red-hot anger at her shooter and icy fear for her suvival.

Jason shook his head. "I'm not going to jail."

Stephen stepped closer. If he could somehow disarm Jason without shooting him—

With the lightning-quick reflexes that had made him a tough opponent at racquetball, Jason whipped the barrel of his pistol against his temple. "I'm not going to jail."

The shot reverberated through the stillness and echoed off the surrounding mountains.

With a look of astonishment, Jason crumpled to the porch.

Stephen knelt beside him. "The baby, Jason. Where is Jessica?"

He felt for a pulse, but Jason's body was already cooling in the frigid night air. With a terrible sense of failure, he shoved to his feet and leaped the steps to where Rachel lay sprawled on the front path.

He knelt and gathered her in one arm, almost sobbing in relief at the warmth of her skin, pulled out his cell phone with his other hand and requested an ambulance and FBI backup from 911.

Rachel stirred and opened her eyes.

"Be still," he ordered. "An ambulance is on the way."

She struggled to sit up and rubbed her chest. "I

don't need an ambulance. My vest stopped the bullet, but I'm going to have a doozie of bruise."

Her glance fell on Jason, lying on the porch. With a cry of distress, she scrambled to her feet and ran toward him. Stephen followed and watched her check the pulse at Jason's neck.

She raised her face to meet Stephen's gaze, and her eyes were wide with panic. "He's dead."

Stephen's stomach knotted. He was sorry for Jason's death, no matter what crimes he'd committed. "He said he wasn't going to jail."

Rachel fought back a heartrending sob. "And now Jessica's lost. We'll never find her in time without Jason to lead us to where she is."

Her daughter—*their* daughter—was somewhere on the mountain, shivering in the cold, at the mercy of the elements and wild animals. With a shudder he remembered the bark they'd heard earlier. Had a wild dog already discovered her?

"We'll find her." Stephen dialed 911 again to ask for a search party. "I promise you, Rachel. I'll find her if it's the last thing I do."

WITHIN TWENTY MINUTES half a dozen agents, who had followed them from the rest area and waited at the Glenville post office, filled the cabin. Rachel stood on the porch, oblivious of the cold, watching the searching beams of flashlights and listening to the shouts of the men who combed the mountainside. Her chest ached from the impact of Jason's bullet, but that pain was insignificant compared to her agony over her missing baby.

Deputies from the Jackson County Sheriff's Office, their tracking dogs and dozens of volunteers searched for Jessica, but it was a big mountain. Covering the entire area would take hours, and with the cold increasing, Jessica wouldn't survive much longer.

Her misery was too deep for tears. If Jessica wasn't found soon...

The door to the cabin opened and closed, and familiar arms surrounded her.

"You'll freeze out here," Stephen said, his breath warm against her face. "Come inside where there's some heat."

"If they won't let me search, the least I can do is keep watch."

He seemed to understand that she wouldn't be swayed. "I've given a full report of what happened to Jack Roche."

"How was Jason Bender mixed up in all this?"

"Jason was the mastermind. He planned the Maitland kidnapping."

"But he was one of *us*. Why would he do such a thing?"

"Greed, envy?" Stephen shrugged. "With Jason dead, we'll never know for sure."

"He didn't really get a call from that informant about Weed and Bubba?"

"Evidently not. After we found Margaret Maitland and she identified her kidnappers, Jason knew he had to kill them to protect himself."

"And Harold Maitland," Rachel said. "Was he involved?"

"According to Jack, Maitland's clean. His New York alibi checks out."

"Did Jason kill Milton Carver?"

He nodded. "Carver and Ralph Fulton both knew about Jason's involvement with Weed and Bubba. For a while, Jason managed to keep them quiet with promises of staging another kidnapping and cutting them in on the big money."

"Then you arrested Milton in Atlanta."

"Milton gave up Jason," Stephen said, "hoping to get a lighter sentence for the arsons he'd committed. But Jason shot him before he could make an official statement."

"You were the only one Milton had talked to?"

"That's why I was such a danger to Jason. He'd already gone to the Okefenokee and shot Ralph Fulton. With me—and you—out of the way, Jason must have figured he'd be safe."

"How did you know he was after me, too?" Rachel asked.

"After Milton Carver was shot in Atlanta, Jason got the drop on me while I was searching for the sniper."

"You talked to him then?"

He nodded. "With my amnesia, I didn't remember until I saw Jason again on the porch here. In Atlanta, he bragged about what he'd done and told me he was going to kill you, too."

"Did he say why?"

"To cover all his tracks. He said since you'd worked the Maitland kidnapping with me, you might be able to figure out his involvement. He couldn't risk letting you live.''

Rachel shook her head in disbelief. ''He wasn't thinking straight. Didn't he know by killing *both* of us, he'd have the Bureau going over every case we ever worked together?''

Stephen tightened his arms around her. ''Jason hadn't been thinking straight for a long time, or he would never have attempted the Maitland kidnapping.''

''Jason was the one who shot you in the arm?''

''After he shot me, I managed to get away. That's when I called you to meet me here.''

Rachel leaned against him. ''So many people dead for one man's greed. And now Jessica—''

Stephen shook her gently. ''We'll find her. I'm going out now to help search.''

''She's so tiny, so helpless.'' Her voice caught in her throat. ''Please find her.''

He turned her to face him, and his dark gaze bore into hers. ''I won't come back without her.''

Before she could speak, he released her and strode off the porch and around the cabin.

The cold ate into her bones, and she tried not to think how icy the ground was or of Jessica lying exposed to the freezing air.

''Cry, Jess,'' she said aloud. ''Scream your tiny lungs out so we can hear you.''

The long minutes dragged by, and still no one returned with her baby. Jack Roche brought her coffee and forced her to drink the hot liquid. The dejected expression on his face told her he knew Jessica's time was running out, but neither of them spoke of it.

The searchers had long ago disappeared over the ridge and out of sight, working their way down the mountain. Occasionally the howl of a bloodhound drifted up the slope, but no one returned with her baby.

Stephen would never forgive her. She had kept his child a secret, and now, before he'd had a chance to know and love her...

Stop it! You can't give up hope.

Rachel was too pragmatic to believe in miracles. It had been more than an hour since the search had begun, closer to two hours since Jason had told them about hiding Jessica. And he had left her on the mountain long before then.

But as much as her practical brain insisted Jessica's time had run out, Rachel refused to believe it in her heart. She would hold her daughter again, see her sunny smile, hear her silly laugh.

She couldn't live if she didn't.

She huddled in despair against a porch post. Gradually, she detected a distant noise, coming from down the mountainside behind the cabin.

The clamor of the engine grew louder.

Suddenly a large tractor chugged around the corner and parked in the front yard. Clayton Jones hopped from the driver's seat and held his arms out to Stephen, who sat perched behind.

Stephen handed Clayton something, hopped to the ground, then retrieved the bundle from the farmer.

Cradling the parcel in his arms, Stephen started up the path toward Rachel.

Rachel's heart froze in her throat.

Stephen had found Jessica, just as he'd promised.

But was she alive?

With a strangled cry, she leaped from the porch and ran to meet him.

"Clayton's German shepherd ran off over an hour ago," Stephen said. "When Clayton found Rusty a few minutes ago, he was curled around Jessica, keeping her warm. Clayton didn't know who she belonged to until he found me searching the mountainside as he was taking her home to call the authorities."

"Is she all right?"

"She's been safe and warm all this time with Rusty."

He folded back the blanket, and Jessica peered out at her with dark eyes so like her father's. Rachel grabbed her daughter and held her close. Over Jessica's short dark curls, Rachel's gaze met Stephen's.

"Thank you." she said. "I hope you can forgive me for not telling you sooner about your daughter."

"We've both made mistakes. That's all behind us now," he said in a voice rough with emotion, and drew them both into his arms. "When I saw you go down from Jason's bullet, I knew then you—and Jessica—were more important to me than anything in the world."

"But—"

With their daughter clutched between them, he dipped his head and kissed her.

A few minutes later he released her, breathless. "Now let's take our daughter home."

"To my house?"

"To *our* house. Remember, we're a family now, and this family's been apart too long already."

Get ready for heart-pounding romance and white-knuckle suspense!

HARLEQUIN®

I N T R I G U E®

raises the stakes in a new miniseries

The McCord family of Texas is in a desperate race against time!

With a killer on the loose and the clock ticking toward midnight, a daughter will indulge in her passion for her bodyguard; a son will come to terms with his past and help a woman with amnesia find hers; an outsider will do anything to save his unborn child and the woman he loves.

With time as the enemy, only love can save them!

#533 STOLEN MOMENTS
B.J. Daniels
October 1999

#537 MEMORIES AT MIDNIGHT
Joanna Wayne
November 1999

#541 EACH PRECIOUS HOUR
Gayle Wilson
December 1999

Available at your favorite retail outlet.

HARLEQUIN®
Makes any time special ™

Amnesia...
an unknown danger...
a burning desire.

With

HARLEQUIN®

I N T R I G U E ®

you're just

A MEMORY AWAY

from passion, danger...and love!

**Look for all the books in this
exciting miniseries:**

**#527 ONE TEXAS NIGHT
by Sylvie Kurtz**
August 1999

**#531 TO SAVE HIS BABY
by Judi Lind**
September 1999

**#536 UNDERCOVER DAD
by Charlotte Douglas**
October 1999

A MEMORY AWAY—where remembering
the truth becomes a matter of life,
death...and love!

Available wherever Harlequin books are sold.

HARLEQUIN®
Makes any time special ™

"This book is DYNAMITE!"
—Kristine Rolofson

"A riveting page turner…"
—Joan Elliott Pickart

"Enough twists and turns to keep everyone guessing… What a ride!"
—Jule McBride

See what all your favorite authors are talking about.

Coming October 1999 to a retail store near you.

HARLEQUIN®
Makes any time special ™

Silhouette®

 **HARLEQUIN®**
Makes any time special ™

WIN A DREAM

In celebration of Harlequin®'s golden anniversary

Enter to win a *dream!* You could win:

- A luxurious trip for two to
  The Renaissance Cottonwoods Resort
  in Scottsdale, Arizona, or

- A bouquet of flowers once a week for a year
  from **FTD**, or

- A $500 shopping spree, or

- A fabulous bath & body gift basket, including
  K-tel's *Candlelight and Romance* 5-CD set.

Look for **WIN A DREAM** flash on
specially marked Harlequin® titles by
Penny Jordan, Dallas Schulze,
Anne Stuart and Kristine Rolofson
in October 1999*.

FTD®

K·TEL

**RENAISSANCE.
COTTONWOODS RESORT**
SCOTTSDALE, ARIZONA

*No purchase necessary—for contest details send a self-addressed envelope to Harlequin Makes Any Time Special Contest, P.O. Box 9069, Buffalo, NY, 14269-9069 (include contest name on self-addressed envelope). Contest ends December 31, 1999. Open to U.S. and Canadian residents who are 18 or over. Void where prohibited.

PHMATS-GR

HARLEQUIN®

I N T R I G U E®

COMING NEXT MONTH

#537 MEMORIES AT MIDNIGHT by Joanna Wayne
The McCord Family Countdown

Darlene Remington couldn't remember who wanted her dead, but she recognized Sheriff Clint Richards easily—she'd walked away from his strong, protective arms six years ago. Seeing Darlene again reminded Clint just how much he needed a woman in his life—Darlene, to be specific. In a race to find her would-be killer, was Clint ready to confront his past...and willing to risk his heart?

#538 NO BABY BUT MINE by Carly Bishop

Thrown together by tragedy, Kirsten McCourt and Garrett Weisz had shared one night of compassion—and pleasure. Five years later, caught in the grasp of a powerful vigilante leader, Kirsten and Garrett are reunited by danger. Determined to keep Kirsten safe and in his life, Garrett will stop at nothing to obtain justice—especially when he finds that her kidnapped son is also his....

#539 FOR HIS DAUGHTER by Dani Sinclair

Accused of his ex-wife's murder, with no memory of the night in question, Officer Lee Garvey turned to Kayla Coughlin for help. Kayla had never trusted the police, but Lee's obvious devotion to his two-year-old daughter made it difficult to believe the man could be capable of murder—and their mutual attraction made him hard to resist....

#540 WHEN NIGHT DRAWS NEAR by Lisa Bingham

When their plane makes an emergency landing in the snowy wilderness of the Rocky Mountains, Elizabeth Boothe and Seth Brody must fight against an unknown killer and the still-smoldering attraction of their failed marriage. Stranded, with only each other to trust, the couple must overcome both danger and desire to make it off the mountain alive....

Look us up on-line at: http://www.romance.net